LANTA: SONG OF THE SEA

Fergus P Egan

LANTA: SONG OF THE SEA

Author and Publisher: Fergus P Egan

ISBN: 978-1-7776037-5-5 (Paperback Edition)
ISBN: 978-1-7776037-6-2 (Hardcover Edition)
ISBN: 978-1-7776037-7-9 (Electronic Book Edition)

Story Development: Aisling Egan

Editor: Andrew Niall Egan

Cover design: Andrew Niall Egan

Photographs: Aisling Egan

DISCLAIMER

ISBN: 978-1-7776037-5-5

Kevin Doherty suffers from enochlophobia – fear of public places. He finds and befriends a lost girl, a survivor of a storm at sea, whom he names 'Lanta'. The ensuing relationship is mutually beneficial to the reclusive man and the foundling. They resolve to remain together. Their relationship is threatened, not by their respective personal struggles, but by an ill-informed society that misunderstands mental illness.

LANTA: SONG OF THE SEA

LIST OF CHIEF CHARACTERS

Lanta
A foundling girl

Kevin Doherty
Former teacher with enochlophobia
(fear of public places)

Fred Harrison
A country doctor and sole friend of Kevin Doherty

Padraig and Maura Doherty
Parents of Kevin Doherty

Seamus O'Dowd
Garda sergeant

Kathleen McBrearty
Doctor of Psychological Science in Clinical Psychology

Brian McCann
Official from the Canadian Consulate

LANTA: SONG OF THE SEA

Fergus P Egan

CHAPTER ONE

FRED HARRISON, M.D.

I, Fred Harrison, M.D., write this account for my private benefit. I fear that someday I will look back and deny what happened. Yes, the incidents undeniably occurred. But the manner and circumstances were strange and mysterious. While the events are still fresh in my mind, I commit them to paper. I say 'fresh in my mind'. I should say 'haunting my restless nights'. The time approaches when I will purge the troubling memories from my mind. This account is for my own eyes only. It is at odds with the official record, not because I misrepresent the truth. Rather, I am unable to fully explain what happened. Nor do I understand. My informed brain struggles with the contradictory experience of my senses. Herein is a record of the life of 'Lanta', a foundling rescued by Kevin Doherty and who lived under his protective care for a brief time.

Some of what I know is from my professional observations. But most is gleaned from my conversations with Kevin Doherty and from his diary. Was he of sound mind when he recorded the events of his isolated life? There is no doubt that he was in grief from an earlier tragedy that drove him to a withdrawn state. And a second tragedy, when it befell him, was too much for him to bear.

Kevin was once my closest friend. In the end, I was his only friend. Sadly, Kevin died more than once. Twice, he died emotionally from grief. And, finally, he died physically – although his body was never found. His life ended in tragedy. But how did it begin?

*   *   *   *   *   *   *

After serving as a military doctor in Afghanistan, I re-entered civilian life. I sought to return to my childhood home in Dunkineely and hoped that my service with the British Army would not be held against me. Four years ago, I secured a practice in Ardara, a 20-minute drive from my family home. I settled comfortably into a country practice. I reconnected with the people I once knew. This brought me to Inver and the nearby Salthill strand, a mere five kilometres from my childhood home. This is where I spent many happy days with Kevin Doherty – five kilometres is a short distance for a boy on a bicycle. Kevin's family owned, and still owns, a pub in Inver. His father was a school inspector, now retired. I remember Kevin playing piano in the pub. He and I would sing in harmony all the popular ballads. Later, we grew up. And grew apart. So upon my return to Donegal, and to satisfy my yearning to reconnect, I visited Inver and enquired of Padraig Doherty about how his son Kevin was faring and how I might contact him. That's when I learned of the tragic turn in Kevin's life.

Kevin had become a teacher. Shortly after obtaining a teaching position, he married a colleague. Seven months later, the couple went on a belated honeymoon to Spain. Sally was four months pregnant at the time. In Spain, Kevin rented a sailboat. And during a manoeuvre at sea, he caused the boom to swing unexpectedly. It struck Sally and knocked her overboard. She died as a result. Although it was ruled an accident, Kevin blamed himself for her death. He fell into depression and lost his job. He retired into seclusion at Maghera. Thereafter, Padraig and Maura would visit him once a month. But he clearly wanted to be alone and the visits were unwelcomed and brief.

Upon learning the news about Kevin, I resolved to locate him. The Maghera that Padraig referred to was Maghera beach and caves, ten kilometres from Ardara and a short drive from my doctor's office. During my service in Afghanistan, I treated post-traumatic stress disorder in soldiers. Surely, back here in Donegal, I could render my professional help to Kevin Doherty.

CHAPTER TWO

THE COTTAGE BY THE SEA

I drove to Maghera. There are six houses in Maghera, with another twenty nearby. It is not a village and has no structured layout. Houses are situated haphazardly on plots of land according to personal whims – close to the twisting road, or along the side of a hill, or for no apparent reason. They are seldom side by side. I approached one house to ask for help in identifying the abode of Kevin Doherty. The kind woman of the house recognized me.

"Doctor Harrison, is it? And what do you be wantin' out here at all, at all?"

I recognized her. "Mrs Bonner? And how are you?"

"I'm fine. How's yourself?"

"I'm fine. I don't need a doctor." We both chuckled. "But I'm not here to see yourself. I'm trying to find Kevin Doherty. I'm told he lives hereabouts."

"Kevin Doherty, the mad fellah is it? What? Have you come to take him away?"

"Ah, Mrs Bonner, I wouldn't call him a 'mad fellah'…"

"Well, we keep far away from him; and him from us.

Sure, the childer are scarred o' him. And meself half-afeared as well."

"That's as well might be, but I'm trying to locate him."

Mrs Bonner grunted to indicate that I was on a futile quest. "If you really want to get to his place you need to go farther out the road, just round the corner there, and take the laneway up and over the hill." She pointed. But there was nothing to see but wind-swept bogland and coastal cliffs.

Perceiving my confusion, the kind woman elucidated. "His place is not visible from the road. And the laneway is overgrown with rushes and moss. But it's there, all right. And it will take your car if you don't mind the rushes brushing you underneath. See where the yon stone wall ends? That's the end of his lane. And if you drive up the lane too far, and pass his cottage, you'll drive off the cliff and into the sea."

I wasn't sure if Mrs Bonner was being dramatic in her descriptive directions. She is given to exaggerating. But just to be sure, I took her literally and drove with caution. I found the laneway where she had indicated. The surface was flagstoned and surfaced with stones, of which there is an abundance at hand. The route was discernible from the growth on the lane's surface – the rushes were high in the centre and the moss was thin in the wheel tracks. I drove slowly in first gear. The loose stones thudded against the undercarriage and the rushes produced a swishing sound. I maneuvered gingerly up the slope. In a short time, I crested the summit and beheld a low cottage close to the edge of the cliff overlooking the crashing waves. The sea breeze carried wayward portions of the spray from the breakers up the cliff face to deposit intermittent sprinkles on the car's windshield. This was Kevin Doherty's place and, like Kevin himself, it was cut off from civilization.

The cottage was a low structure with a rounded corrugated-tin roof. This was once a common shape for buildings in windswept coastal locations. The walls were constructed of local stone, grey and drab. And one would need to stoop to enter through the doorway. I wondered why a cottage would be built here, in this forlorn place. Certainly, it was hidden from places of human habitation and activity. Concealed from human eyes, yes, but exposed to the elements. I was surprised that it was devoid of a windbreak of shrubbery. But judging from the blasted landscape, I surmised that the prevailing salt-laden wind had scorched all vegetation to stunted stubbles. Only coarse grass, bleached white, struggled to survive amongst the thickets of heather. There was a pervading smell of wrack and seaweed. And the incessant sound of the turbulent sea intruded unchecked.

I later learned that there is a pathway from the cottage to the shore. The pathway leads to a sheltered cove suitable for mooring a small boat. But there is no pier there. The pathway also extends to the beach and the caves. There is no other suitable mooring location in the sea inlet at Maghera. Nor is there one in the next inlet up the coast. The closest pier is at Rossbeg on the Magheragallon peninsula, a half-hour drive away. Or alternatively, at Port Pier down the coast past the Knockfola headland, also a half-hour drive. Notwithstanding, boating is safe at Maghera if one stays within the inlet. The sandbars subdue the Atlantic rollers. Beyond the sandbars and past the headland of Knockfola, the ocean is rough. Furthermore, the currents are treacherous rounding the headland. To safely leave or enter the inlet, one needs to ride the tides in a boat fit for the sea – easy for a knowledgeable and experienced boatman.

I approached the solitary cottage and parked the car. I saw another car parked at the side. I noticed the absence of smoke from the chimney. Mixed signals – someone is here; no one is here. I knocked at the door. No one answered. I knocked harder. The door swung open a fraction with a perceptible squeak. Still no response. I peered into the gloomy interior of the cottage. It took a moment to adjust my eyes to the dim light. I saw him – or someone. Was this Kevin Doherty? A man with the appearance of an emaciated vagabond sat on a chair facing a dead fire. I shivered at the sight. It was like viewing a zombie in a scene from the '*Night of the Living Dead*'. Dispensing with propriety, I entered the house and strode to the man.

"Kevin? Is that you?"

He looked at me sluggishly and said, "Yes. And who are you?"

"It's me, Fred. You know? Your harmony singer from way back – Fred Harrison."

"Oh, yes. So, it is." His eyes registered recognition for an instant and then resumed a tired stare. "Hello, Fred."

I realized that vital action was required. Kevin Doherty was hungry and dirty. And he had no motivation to move. The place smelled like a pigsty and the dead fire released a pong of wet soot. I took stock of the situation. There was no food in the house, although there was a collection of empty bean cans littering the floor in the kitchen. I filled a bucket from the outside well and gave Kevin a cup of water. He drank it slowly. Then he asked for more. The entire house was devoid of all the essentials for living. There was no turf for the fire. The gas cylinders were exhausted, so the gas cooker was not functioning. Kevin's car was parked outside at the gable-end of the cottage. I conducted a quick examination. The key was in the ignition. I immediately determined that the battery was flat and that the petrol tank was likely empty.

I drove back to the main road, to the Texaco service station in Drumbaran on the outskirts of Ardara. I purchased tins of beans and sardines, bread, a full cylinder of gas and a bag of turf. An hour after I had first entered the cottage, I was busy preparing a hot meal for Kevin – beans on toast and sardines on toast. I had forgotten to buy butter and condiments, including tea and sugar. Nevertheless, Kevin consumed the meal. This revived him. His strength returned. He questioned me as to why I had come to visit. I told him a story to distract him. Meanwhile, I took him into the scullery. The scullery was equipped for cleaning vegetables and laundering clothes. It even had a fireplace with pots for boiling sheets in 'blue' to bleach them. The only thing missing was a mangle. I went to work on Kevin. Utilizing water from the rain barrel, I bathed him and shaved him. I found clean clothes for him to wear. And I bundled his dirty clothes to take to the laundry in Ardara. When I was finished, Kevin looked like a healthy human being again – albeit, a bit too thin. Thankfully, he no longer smelled like a pig in muck.

Taking care of Kevin was my priority over the

following days. It took a week to get his living routine back in order. On subsequent visits, I stocked his larder with potatoes, salt and pepper, tea and sugar. I arranged with Mrs Bonner to provide him with milk and eggs daily. This was a challenge. She refused to come to the 'mad fellah's' cottage. Instead, she agreed to fill his milk jug if he placed it on the gatepost. I didn't know Kevin even had a gatepost until I looked for one. In the past, his front yard had been enclosed. But the wall was gone; the gate was missing. The only things that remained were two stone pillars standing like sentries at the end of his lane. As to eggs – the hens don't always lay well. So, Mrs Bonner agreed to place two eggs daily in summer; later, one egg. And when the hens stop laying, the frequency would drop. At the end of the week, I was satisfied that Kevin's diet was sufficient for his health and that it required minimal cooking skills. If Kevin was competent enough to light the gas, he could boil water; boil eggs and potatoes; heat his beans and sardines; wet his tea. Amongst the papers strewn on the table by the window, I found his mobile cell phone. It was no surprise to see that the battery had run down. And since there was no electricity in the cottage, I took the phone and later charged it in my office. In the second week, we got his car running again. My next priority was to concentrate on his rehabilitation.

CHAPTER THREE

REHABILITATION

In the first few days at Maghera, I spent dedicated time with Kevin to ensure that his health was recovering. In my daily visits, I prompted him to bestir himself to be self-reliant. Left to himself, Kevin did not accomplish anything. He neglected to collect his daily milk from the gatepost; he failed to keep the fire alight and he had no motivation to cook food. On the other hand, he reacted positively to my prompting. He brewed a pot of tea for me when I requested it. I searched for some task or responsibility that he might undertake on his own. The answer came to me in the assortment of papers on his table.

"Kevin. I see a lot of paper on your table. Are you writing something?"

From his chair at the fireplace, he looked over at the table by the window. "Am I writing something? No. I was going to start but…"

"What did you intend to write?"

"I don't remember. I don't suppose it was important. Anyhow, I didn't write a single stroke."

"Well, here's a thing you can do for me. You see, I need to keep track of things here – just to be sure that things go right for you." I lifted a clean jotter and wrote a heading on the first page – DAILY JOURNAL. I entered the date on the second line. I passed the jotter to Kevin with a request. "Kevin, I want you to record what you do each day. Can you do that for me?"

"Oh, I suppose I can." Kevin's response was a dismissal. It was clear that he had no intention of fulfilling my request.

On the following day, I queried Kevin about his journal. The page for the intended entry was blank. "So, Kevin, what did you do yesterday that you could enter in the journal?"

Kevin shifted in his chair and grunted a muffled word. "Nothing."

I passed the journal to him and handed him a pen. "So, write 'Nothing'."

He reluctantly did as I asked.

A day later, I viewed his journal again. This time, he had entered one word voluntarily – 'Nothing'. I passed the journal to him and smiled. "You got that wrong, Kevin. You wrote the word 'Nothing' in your journal. But you made an actual entry. And that's something."

Kevin smiled weakly at the joke.

"Tell you what, Kevin. Why don't I suggest a task for you? When you fulfill the task, you record it in your journal."

Kevin looked at me to determine if I were serious. He nodded half-heartedly and said, "I suppose."

And that is how the journal entries started. I suggested tasks and Kevin performed them. At the end of each day, he wrote an account in his journal. Very soon, I had Kevin performing the routine household tasks and recording them in his diary. He also got inventive in his writings. Instead of detailing a description of repetitive tasks day after day, he assigned a code with an explanatory cross-reference. I understood the code. I could tell from the written characters that he lit the fire, fetched the milk, cooked his dinner or whatever.

A week later, after he had diligently recorded his everyday jobs, I read a surprising entry – 'made soup'. I queried Kevin on the novel entry. He explained that he had been mashing his boiled potatoes, into which he threw in a dollop of butter for flavour. And to produce a creamier result, he poured in a generous helping of milk. He misjudged the amount. The result was a liquid mix of milk and potatoes. I was about to say 'too bad', but Kevin boasted that the result was pleasant. He added this newly-discovered milky potato soup to his limited selection of food dishes. I considered the dish a disaster, but if it made Kevin happy, then it was a success. His circle of interest was widening. Thereupon, I decided to strike while the iron was hot.

"Kevin, me boyo," I said. "Try to surprise me a second time. I bet you can't."

He pointed his finger at me in a mock threat and said, "Come back tomorrow."

Kevin was true to his word. A day later, the journal contained another surprising entry – 'Went for a walk to the beach.' It pleased me to learn that Kevin was pulling himself together. A walk on the beach was a sign that he was forming a positive outlook. I attempted to learn more about his outdoor experience. "A walk on the beach? That's great. Did you meet any of your neighbours on your venture?"

"Neighbours? Hah! I made sure to stay out of sight. I accessed the beach by the pathway down the cliff."

This is when I first learned of the pathway. "There is a pathway in the cliff face?"

"Right here at the house. Come, I'll show you."

Kevin walked me to the edge of the cliff. He pointed to the jagged cliff face. The cliff face is not a sheer drop. It is broken and gouged by erosion. But, I was unable to discern any 'pathway'. Kevin proceeded to walk. I followed him. He picked his way down the rocky slope until we reached a hidden cove in a crevice of the rock face. The floor of the crevice sloped gently to the beach. This, he informed me, was once active as a slipway for mooring a small boat, back when it was employed to great advantage by smugglers. I looked around. I agreed that the pathway from the cottage to the beach was well hidden from prying eyes and nosy neighbours.

We made our way back to the cottage. I was panting from the exertion and was relieved to stand on flat ground again. Kevin was talkative. This was a positive sign that he was coming out of himself. He continued to describe his venture. "As I said, I kept well out of sight of the neighbours. And to be certain, I made the trek at midnight."

I held my breath upon hearing this. It was foolhardy to descend the cliff face at any time – the 'pathway' is rough and sloped; the wind from the sea tears across the exposed rocks. But worse, to perform the journey at night was downright reckless. I composed myself and concealed my disapproval. On the positive side, I considered Kevin's progress. I decided to take another step forward in his rehabilitation – a more prudent step than his midnight ramble. I made my move. "Kevin, let's take a drive tomorrow. We'll go in your car. You'll be able to charge your phone as you drive."

"Me drive?" He was surprised, but not ill-disposed to the suggestion. "And sure, where would we drive to? I am content staying around here."

"I was thinking of you driving to the service station to buy your groceries. We could go together."

He nodded slowly. "I suppose that would be all right." Then he looked at me and said, "Except, I am all out of money."

"What? You've no money?"

"Oh, I have money all right. But it's in the bank. It's in my account in the Ulster Bank in Ardara. I don't like to go in there. There's always a queue. And the teller asks questions and… I don't have money for shopping."

Kevin displayed the symptoms of enochlophobia. At first, I considered agoraphobia – a fear of crowds. But Kevin dreaded public places in which people might gather. He was apprehensive at the **possibility** of a crowd, not just the **presence** of a crowd. A trusted companion at his side, however, could significantly alleviate the fear. I planned to accompany Kevin to places where there was no risk of encountering a crowd. I made preparations for the strategic outing.

The day's outing started with a mixture of caution and optimism. Kevin dressed appropriately in a hoodie that concealed his face. His eyes peered tentatively from the shadow of the hood. He drove his car to the main road. Meanwhile, his mobile phone was charged in the armrest. We reached the Texaco station. Kevin stopped the car at the entrance to the shop. We sat and observed the activity. Most people drove up to the petrol pumps and executed their purchases by swiping a credit card. Others entered the shop and paid at the checkout, usually with an added purchase of cigarettes or lottery tickets. Very few entered the grocery area of the shop. It contained islands of shelving for self-service – and lots of display stands to hide behind. Kevin was satisfied that there was little risk of encountering unwanted people in the shop. We entered. Kevin selected his purchases quickly and with little forethought – tins of beans and sardines, bread and butter. I slipped him a 20-Euro bill and directed him to the cashier. He wordlessly placed his chosen items on the counter and placed his money alongside. The cashier gave the customary greeting without attempting eye contact. He registered the sale and tendered the change to Kevin. We exited the shop with our purchases without incident. Kevin expressed satisfaction.

The next stop was the bank. I assured Kevin that I had made an appointment with the branch manager. There was no risk of encountering people, queues or an inquisitive teller. Kevin was uneasy with the prospect. However, he trusted me. The visit to the bank was trying but workable. Kevin succeeded in withdrawing €1,000 in cash and obtained an activity printout of the account. He had a healthy balance in his account thanks to the monthly allowance deposited by his family in Inver.

The third and final stop was to be the most challenging. We entered Hughie McHugh's barbershop. There was a customer in the barber chair and two more waiting. The talk was loud and friendly. Hughie made a humorous comment and everyone laughed. But when we entered, the company went quiet. Everyone looked at Kevin briefly and thereafter averted their eyes. I signalled to Hughie with my eyebrows. He understood.

Hughie slapped his current customer on the shoulder and exclaimed, "There you go. All done. Your wife won't recognize you." The man vacated the chair and paid the fee. Hughie turned to Kevin and said, "You're next."

Kevin hesitated. He realized that two customers were ahead of him.

Hughie gestured in the direction of the two waiting men. "Oh, don't mind those two oul codgers. Sure they're only in here to pass the time. You'd think they had no homes to go to." He swivelled the chair and invited Kevin to sit. He slid the hoodie back and studied Kevin's untidy hair. "And who cut your hair last? Someone with a mowing machine? Well, don't you worry. I'll have you looking like a politician in two shakes of a lamb's tail."

The experience did not go well. Kevin was acutely aware of the silence of the two waiting customers. They coughed occasionally and moved their feet. Kevin shifted his weight in the chair. He squirmed and held his head at the wrong angle. I could see an imminent panic attack. I signalled Hughie to complete the process. Hughie concluded the haircut before it was fully executed. It was the worst job he had ever performed. I quickly tendered the fee, with a grateful tip, and we hastily left the shop.

Outside, Kevin was distraught. He refused to sit in the driver's seat of the car. This meant that I would be required to drive the car for the remainder of the trip. I needed to come up with something to counteract his obvious distress. The shop next to Hughie's had fish for sale. I remembered that it was salmon season. I entered the shop and purchased four salmon steaks.

Back in the car, Kevin muttered, "I want to go. Don't stop anywhere. Just take me home." He pulled his hood further down to cover his face and bent his head. We drove in silence.

Upon reaching the cottage, Kevin plonked himself in his customary chair by the fire. I threw a few sods of turf on the embers and coaxed a welcoming flame. Thereafter, I lit the gas stove and fried the salmon steaks in butter. I regretted the absence of deep-fried potatoes and peas. And there was no mayonnaise for garnish. I made do with butter, salt and pepper. I hoped that the treat would please Kevin and draw him out of his depression. I made room to dine at his table. I pushed his papers and books to one side and placed two plates of salmon in the cleared area. I invited Kevin to partake. He ignored me. His attention was focused on the flickering flames. I tried to make light of the situation by speaking to the empty chair at the table. "Fresh Atlantic Salmon. It's at its best at this time of year. Now be careful of the salmon bones. You don't want to choke on one and die."

"Cormac Mac Airt." Kevin uttered these words unexpectedly. At least he was talking again.

I responded. "What about Cormac Mac Airt?"

"Cormac Mac Airt was High King. He choked to death on a salmon bone."

I knew the legend. But I encouraged Kevin to continue. "How do you know about Cormac Mac Airt?"

"There is a book beside you on the table – *Irish Myths and Legends*." Kevin rose from his chair by the fire and walked to the table. He placed his finger on a book at my elbow. "Page 96. That's where you'll find the story." He tapped his finger a few times. Then he continued. "This is a schoolbook. It is the English Reader for Fourth Class. I once used it to teach children."

I feigned surprise. "And what else is in the book?"

Kevin sat down at his place at the table and started to nibble at his portion of salmon. "Tales of Irish heroes – Fionn Mac Cumhaill, Cú Chulainn, all of them."

In the end, it was a successful day. Thereafter, although not cured of his phobia, Kevin was able to function on his own. He frequently drove unaccompanied to the Texaco service station to obtain his household supplies and food. He settled on a limited diet – potatoes, milky potato soup, beans and sardines on toast, eggs and strong tea. He went walking every day. He frequently hiked, on one or more of his indiscernible paths, to the cliffs of Knockfola headland. There, he surveyed the seascape. Gull Island, tall and craggy, lay to the west. It looked as if it had just detached from the rock face of the headland. Fourteen kilometres to the north, beyond Magheragallon peninsula, lay Roaninish, a low-lying rocky islet at the mouth of Gweebarra Bay, that looked like it had recently surfaced from beneath the sea.

Kevin wrote multiple pages in his journal daily. He developed four distinct styles. Some entries were written as for an instruction manual – brief and to the point. There was his flowery prose and poetic descriptions of the constantly changing landscape and seascape he beheld every day. Thirdly, he developed an indecipherable coded language. The 'words' were comprised of shapes and spirals. I wondered if they were meaningless doodles and if Kevin himself understood their meaning. He was eager for me to read his journal when I visited him, but he never tendered an explanation of his coded language. The fourth style was a later development. It speculated on catastrophes that would render Kevin the sole remaining human on earth. One such piece addressed his survival if a comet hit the earth and destroyed life on the surface of the planet. Would it trigger a sudden evolutionary response from life in the oceans? Perhaps the octopus might emerge as the planet's most intelligent resident? Or perhaps marine mammals would become earthbound and replace the extinct human race? And throughout it all, Kevin himself would be an engaging witness. It was fantasy, of course. Kevin, perchance, might have developed a talent for writing sci-fi in the manner of H. G. Wells.

Notwithstanding the positive progress, Kevin was not cured of his phobia. He functioned satisfactorily despite it. And he was no more 'odd' than many Irish people who live in solitude. He bothered no one, and no one bothered him. He lived a healthy life when left alone. If 'happiness' is defined as 'contentment', rather than a fun-fair rollercoaster ride with ice cream and candy, this could be the end of the story – 'and they all lived happily ever after'.

Unfortunately, this is not the end of the story. The tale has not yet begun.

CHAPTER FOUR

JETSAM FROM THE SEA

Kevin Doherty's health continued to improve. He still suffered from his phobia, but he established effective ways of avoiding groups of people. He still recoiled from physical touching. So, he never undertook a return visit to Hughie the barber. He groomed his long hair into a ponytail. An overdue visit to the dentist was delayed indefinitely. He continued to obtain his everyday essentials at the convenience store attached to the petrol station.

When the Covid 19 pandemic struck the region, I was concerned about Kevin's reaction and how he would cope with the restrictive regulations. Ironically, the restrictions liberated him. He welcomed the ban on gatherings. Due to social-distancing rules, public places were less daunting to him. Mask-wearing provided added psychological distancing. He successfully conducted business at the bank where a 'one-customer-at-a-time' policy was mandated. The most useful bonus was in remote shopping with roadside pickup. Kevin, who did not possess a computer, ordered purchases by phone and collected his items with minimal person-to-person interaction. Whereas his behaviour was previously regarded as odd, he became a recognized proponent of prudent social distancing. During this period, he added to his collection of clothing and hiking boots. One thing that did not change was his lack of cooking skills. His diet never changed. Once, he invited his parents to visit. They went walking on the beach and viewed the sea caves. He later treated them to 'tea-and-toast'. And since he never cleared his table, the meal was consumed 'on the lap'.

My daily visits to Kevin quickly dropped to weekly visits. The daily calls had become a strain on my professional schedule. After all, I had other patients to tend to and a clinic to manage. So, in time, my visits to Kevin dropped to a monthly schedule but with frequent intervening phone conversations. Kevin had learned to live a satisfying life despite his unrelenting phobia. He was content to live in peaceful seclusion.

Storms are common in the Atlantic. They frequently hammer the coast but quickly lose potency inland. During a particularly fierce storm, I wondered how Kevin was faring. I was satisfied that his cottage was strong enough to survive, considering that it had endured the coastal winds for over one hundred years. At 6:13 am one morning, I was awakened from sleep by the ringing phone. It was Kevin. He was distraught about the aftermath of a storm. He referred to 'jetsam'. He begged me to come urgently to the cottage.

It takes 20 minutes to drive to Kevin's cottage. As I approached Assaranca Waterfall, two kilometres shy of the cottage, the road was littered with wrack washed in from the inlet. I deduced that a spring tide had coincided with the storm. Upon reaching the cottage, I entered without knocking. I expected to witness Kevin having a panic attack or some emotional trauma. I was surprised to see him sitting calmly at his table with pen in hand, presumably writing his journal. The fire was blazing. His wet clothes were draped over chairs by the fire. Steam wafted from them. I did not know whether I should be relieved or annoyed.

"Kevin!" I addressed him loudly. "I thought you said it was urgent."

He pressed his forefinger to his lips and said, "Shush. Keep your voice down." He waited until I settled. Then he continued. "It **is** urgent. But the panic is over."

"So, you had a panic attack?"

"Stop interrupting. Let me tell you." He wrote a few words in his journal, perhaps to finish a sentence, then he laid the pen on the desk. He resumed speaking. "When the storm abated, I decided to go beachcombing…"

"Searching for flotsam and jetsam. What is urgent about that?"

Kevin was irritated by the second interruption. He rose

from the chair and walked to his bedroom. He leaned against the jamb of the open doorway and spoke with noticeable annoyance. "If you are going to keep interrupting, you'll never learn of the urgent matter I summoned you for. Read the journal. That will be quicker. I'll be inside my bedroom waiting for you when you are ready."

He entered the room and left the door wide open. I heard the squeak of the mattress as he sat or lay on his bed. It was evident that Kevin was upset. But he was surprisingly calm. The answer to his peculiar behaviour ostensibly lay in his journal. I proceeded to read the recent entry. I quickly scanned down the page, speed-reading as fast as I could. I identified keywords such as 'wet pathway', 'seaweed', 'cave' and 'jetsam'. I hesitated. Had I misread a passage? I moved my eyes up a few lines to inspect an arresting inscription. I read it slowly and accurately. It described an incident in detail. Here is the passage, paraphrased: Kevin entered the largest of the caves, as he often did. It was past sunrise, but the interior of the cave was as dark as black velvet. As was his practice, he waited to adjust his eyes to the darkness. In a short time, he distinguished the glistening walls, still wet from the high tide. He strode to the rear wall of the cave to look back towards the entrance. From this angle, he would see the silhouette image of anything unfamiliar. He perceived a shape similar to the many rounded rocks on the cave floor, except that it was not present at his visit on the previous day. Could this rock have been placed by the recent tide? It was more likely that it was something other than a rock. Kevin investigated the object intending to drag it out of the cave and into the light. He first determined how heavy it was and if he could get an adequate grip. It was soft to the touch. A gym bag perhaps? Or a drowned dog? He drew his hands across the object, feeling it with his fingers. He identified a head and a spine. He drew back in shock. He composed himself and resumed his inspection. He identified arms, buttocks, and legs. It was the body of a child. He lifted it gently. He detected breathing. The child was alive. Once he exited the cave it was clear that he held a small girl in his arms. She was naked and cold. But she breathed steadily. He quickly removed his jacket and formed it into a pouch. He placed the girl inside the makeshift cradle and tied it around his neck. Thus laden, he climbed the cliff.

At this point, I stopped reading. This was shocking news. And yes, it was urgent. I spoke to Kevin, not sure how to form my words. "You found a girl washed in from the sea? From the storm? And the high tide? Where…?"

Kevin came to the bedroom entrance. He signalled to

me to be quiet. "In here," he whispered. "She is jetsam, a waif from the sea."

I followed his gesture and entered the room lightly. A child lay on the bed, wrapped in a blanket. Her dark head protruded from the folds. She breathed steadily in sleep. I asked a redundant question. "Is this the child you found? The one cast up by the tide? Maybe she was already there, placed in the cave before the storm."

"No. I entered the cave before the tide flowed and immediately after the tide ebbed. She was not there before the high tide. But she **was** there when the tide retreated."

"Then she could only have been deposited by the tidal surge."

"Precisely. This is a jetsam waif. You are a doctor."

I understood the reason why Kevin summoned me. I returned to my car and obtained my medical bag. Back in the bedroom, I proceeded with a medical examination of the child. I determined that she was in good physical health. She shifted once during the examination, but she did not awaken. Had she had any broken bones, sprains or bruising, she would have reacted to the discomfort of my probing. I estimated that she was a tweeny – 10 to 12 years old. Her hair was straight and black. Her body was tanned. It did not display a tan line, so I conjectured that it was her natural skin colour. I looked at Kevin and asked, "And this is how you found her? Unclothed? No swimsuit? No jewellery? No personal items?"

"Just as you see her. So, is she okay?"

"Physically, yes. But I need to examine her further when she is awake. Concussion, emotional damage, trauma etc. Such a girl would not be alone. So, where is her family?"

"And where is she from? She doesn't look Irish."

I could have answered that not all Irish are white. But it was not the time for idle speculation. I phoned the guards and asked to speak with Sergeant Seamus O'Dowd. I gave him a ten-word summary, enough to warrant his presence. Twenty minutes later, Sergeant O'Dowd entered the cottage. I brought him to the bedroom and pointed to the girl.

O'Dowd acknowledged the girl. "So, this is the child you say was washed up by the tide? And you found her in the big cave and brought her here?"

Kevin gave him a detailed account. Throughout, O'Dowd shook his head and muttered, "Poor thing." After hearing Kevin's account, he queried me about the medical examination. I gave him my diagnosis. He pondered for a while. Then he said, "She'll need to be placed with Children's Services until we locate her family."

I objected. "Let's wait until she wakens. I have not finished my examination. She is safe here for now. Moving her at this time is not in her best interests."

O'Dowd looked at me and cast his eyes around the cottage. He asked me to step outside the cottage. He whispered to me so that Kevin could not hear, "You can't leave a young girl in the house with, with… You know, Kevin Doherty's not right in the head."

I objected to the sergeant's judgment. "First off, I intend to remain here until I am satisfied that the child is in good health and in good hands. Secondly, Kevin Doherty was a renowned teacher before he developed his current phobia. He is fearful of crowds, not of a solitary child. From his previous experience, he is well equipped to relate to a child."

"You say he is good with children. Perhaps you are correct. Regardless, I'll run a background check on him with his former school. If he checks out, I'll be satisfied. Until then, the child's in your care."

"As I say, I will remain here until I am satisfied."

"Good. But she will be moved to Children's Services as soon as I can arrange it. It is the obligatory procedure in cases such as this."

"Is it, indeed? As you say. However, I presume that you are going to trace her family through reports of missing children."

"Of course."

"Well, as soon as she is awake, she might be able to tell us about herself."

"I know that. And that is why I'll be back early tomorrow. However, there is one thing I require at this time – a saliva swab for DNA analysis."

"Good thinking. I can get you a sample while she is still asleep."

Later, Sergeant O'Dowd left with the DNA sample. He entered his car. He remarked to me as he shifted into gear, "Keep this quiet. I don't want reporters or snooping neighbours descending on the place. They'll be asking questions we cannot answer. And it would be upsetting to the child." He eased up on the clutch and the car moved forward.

I remarked, "Don't worry about that. Kevin Doherty's cottage is the one place no one visits. And he, sure as hell, does not associate with the rest of the human race – save for myself."

Back in the cottage, I settled into a chair by the fire. Kevin was busy in the kitchen, cooking his customary milk-and-potato soup. I dozed off. I awoke a short time later. I was aware of activity in the bedroom. I stealthily peeked in. Kevin and the girl sat side by side on the bed. I beheld Kevin spoon-feeding soup to her. She drank it greedily. When it was consumed Kevin rose to replenish the bowl. This is when they observed me peering in from the outer room. Upon seeing me, the girl shrieked and ran. With nowhere to hide, she darted from wall to wall and eventually buried herself against Kevin's chest. He covered her with the blanket to conceal her. I observed her hands gripping his back intensely. Kevin shifted with the pain of her piercing fingernails. Notwithstanding, he cradled her concealed body in a protective hug. Sensing that I was not approaching, she relaxed and peered out from under the blanket. She eventually accepted my presence, provided I came no closer. Her brown eyes still viewed me with apprehension.

As the morning progressed, Kevin fed her more soup. Later, she consumed a sardine sandwich but she declined a helping of beans. Whenever Kevin was absent from her, she whined pitifully. I had to postpone any further medical examination. As the day progressed, she tolerated me in the room. Kevin sat by the fire, still cradling her. She appreciated the warmth but was nervous about the flickering flames. She displayed a healthy appetite. She consumed lots of milk, potatoes and sardines.

I phoned Sergeant O'Dowd with an update. He confirmed that he would visit the following morning. He was still working on matching the girl with reports of missing children. He inquired if I had ascertained the girl's name. I explained that she was awake and eating but, so far, she had not spoken. I reminded him that I would remain at the cottage until I had conducted a thorough medical examination. Since an overnight stay was likely, I requested two camp cots. I knew that Sergeant O'Dowd promoted youth camping outings and had access to fold-up cots. He agreed. And since I needed to replenish Kevin's larder, the sergeant delivered the cots to the Texaco station where I picked them up an hour later.

Throughout the day, Kevin attended to the waif. She remained close to him – and distant from me. She had an aversion to wearing clothes. She kicked off her blanket. She covered herself only as a protective measure whenever I moved about the room. I was intrigued by her lack of modesty. She displayed a child-like innocence. This conduct in a 12-year-old is uncharacteristic of a conservative Irish upbringing. Her skin colour, features and conduct suggested that she was from a non-Irish culture. But from where? Had she but spoken a word, I could have derived a clue. When I had the chance, I studied her tan skin colour and physical features. Where was she from? Was she of Mediterranean or Middle-Eastern extraction? It was unlikely that she was sub-Saharan African. Possibly, she was from India. Her face suggested oriental characteristics. I figured that the Philippines or Polynesia was the most likely place of origin. I admitted that this was groundless speculation on my part – I just did not know. She consumed more soup and sardine sandwiches. And she slept on and off for the remainder of the day.

At day's end, I phoned Sergeant O'Dowd with an update. I had no further news for him – the girl appeared healthy; she was eating and sleeping. It is possible she had not eaten for days. And no, I had not conducted my follow-up examination. And no, she had not spoken. O'Dowd, however, had good news to impart. Regarding Kevin Doherty's background check, the headmaster of his previous school described his conduct as 'exemplary'. He was a highly respected teacher. He exhibited extraordinary skills with children, frequently motivating them to excel. He was a great loss to the school when he left due to ill health.

I awoke early the following morning. I don't believe I slept much during the night. The camp cot was too small and uncomfortable. It would not induce me to go camping. I looked for Kevin. He was snugly asleep within the blanket of the second cot which he had placed partway into the bedroom. The sleeping girl, however, was also on the cot. She lay, uncovered, on top of the clothes alongside him. I decided to keep this scene a secret from Sergeant O'Dowd. He would have regarded it as improper. I entered the kitchen in silence and heated the pot of soup. The milky potato soup had become Kevin's standard breakfast, in preference to oatmeal porridge which he disliked. His one or two daily eggs were never present until he went to collect them later in the morning. Regardless, the girl seemed to like the soup. I brought two steaming bowls to the sleeping duo. They both awoke and drank the warm brew bleary-eyed. On this occasion, the girl did not retreat from me. By the time she registered my presence, I had resumed the accepted 'safe distance'. I attempted to conduct an examination. Kevin understood my intentions and cooperated. I swung a watch before the girl's face. She followed the movements correctly. I clicked my fingers at her left ear and at her right ear. Good reaction. I checked her reflexes. She objected mildly and was assuaged by Kevin. She complied. I told her to open her mouth and say 'Ah'. Of course, she did not understand. So, I demonstrated with my mouth wide open. "Ah." Kevin mimicked me with another 'Ah'. We laughed. The girl also laughed and uttered the sound with an open mouth. She objected to the invasive wooden tongue depressor. But I succeeded with the examination. Kevin and I both laughed. I stuck a tongue depressor into his mouth too and we laughed again. The girl was puzzled, but she laughed feebly at the joke she did not understand.

I went to the table and wrote my notes. The girl had understood my request to say 'Ah'. And she complied. She could speak. This was significant. Kevin agreed. He was playing with the child as one would play with a baby, gently poking her and singing a nonsense song. He was coaxing her to speak. He was lilting *'Twinkle. Twinkle Little Star'* in falsetto. She responded to his 'la-lahs' with 'ah-ahs' in the correct pitch and with the correct melody. I was captivated by this. Kevin continued with the melody but substituted the words 'I wonder if my flotsam talks, can she speak a word for me.' This confused her. The game was over for now. But I could see that Kevin, the skilled teacher, was planning something.

Sergeant O'Dowd arrived. He knocked at the front door. "It's me, Sergeant O'Dowd. May I come in?"

Upon hearing the booming voice, the girl panicked and ran into the bedroom. O'Dowd entered the house and stood in the front room. The girl saw him through the open bedroom door. She screamed and threw herself against the wall repeatedly. It was clear that she was terrified of Sergeant O'Dowd.

I shouted at the sergeant. "Get Out! Get out before she injures herself." I turned him around and pushed him back outside. "Can't you see she's terrified of you?"

O'Dowd was so surprised by the girl's reaction that he did not resist me. He complied readily. Outside, we both leaned against the wall of the cottage. We listened to the girl's screams. They abated and were replaced by deep rhythmic sobbing. Kevin could be heard comforting the girl with 'there, there' and audible sounds of patting.

O'Dowd turned to me and asked, "Is she like this all the time? Screaming and injuring herself like that?"

"Lord, no. This is the first time I've witnessed it. And I've been here the whole time, except for the quick visit to the filling station – gone for 20 minutes, 25 at most. Actually, up until you came, her conduct was normal – well, acceptable under the circumstances."

"Normal, you say?"

"She was eating well. I managed to get close to her without upsetting her. I even got her to laugh at one point. And Kevin got her singing along with 'Twinkle, twinkle'."

"Laughing and singing, eh? But not talking?"

"Sergeant, she was coming along fine. That is until you turned up. Something about you set her off – your voice, your bearing, your uniform."

"Are you saying that I frightened her?"

"Your very presence terrified her. Probably, a reminder of a past traumatic experience. It would be in her best interests if you refrained from coming here for a few days. I will remain. I'll phone you periodically with a progress report on her condition. I feel that we are close to having her talking. She reacted favourably to my instructions when I told her to open her mouth and say 'Ah'."

"Reacted favourably? How favourably?"

"When I instructed her to open her mouth and say 'Ah', well, she opened her mouth and said 'Ah'. Undoubtedly, she has the power of speech."

"Well from the sounds of her screams, I agree that she has the power of speech."

"Listen, Sergeant, if we uncover any clues to her identity, I will contact you immediately. As to her identity, have you learned anything from your inquiries?"

"No. No leads at this time. We must glean information from the girl if we are to reunite her with her kin. Now here's a thing you can do for me. Capture images of her on my phone. I will circulate her description to An Garda Siochana and Police Services. Here, take my phone."

I took a series of pictures of the girl on the sergeant's smartphone. I was unable to get a happy image. She appeared sorrowful in every picture. Armed with this material, the sergeant departed from the scene.

A few hours later, the girl appeared joyful again. Kevin was playing a new game with her. I deduced that it was an educational exercise. He encouraged her to sing scales at varying pitches, using a variety of syllables – 'la-lah', and doo-doo', and 'me-me' and so on. She understood and complied happily.

I left the house in mid-afternoon. I was confident that the girl was in good hands. I, on the other hand, had patient visits and clinic appointments to honour. And I needed to sleep in a real bed that night.

Late in the day, Sergeant O'Dowd phoned. He suggested that we meet to discuss the living arrangements for the girl. Since I was already in town, I went to the garda station. When I entered his office he said, "Have a seat." I sat facing him. But his attention was focused on his desktop computer. He appeared to be reading a file as he addressed me. "Captain Frederick Harrison, British Army, served in Afghanistan."

I did not comment.

He continued. "I spoke with the Garda National Immigration Bureau."

"What? On my citizen status?"

O'Dowd laughed and looked me in the eyes. "No. They updated me on the requirements regarding separated children. There is a thing called 'pre-foster care placement.' It is temporary accommodation for a separated child under certain circumstances. We, and that includes me, agree that the foundling girl should remain under your medical care, for the moment."

"What do you mean 'for the moment'?"

"There are strict conditions. One, that you qualify as a temporary guardian; two, that you report daily on her condition; three, the decision rests with Child

Protection and Welfare."

"Child Protection and Welfare? Yes. I see that. And that would be Tusla, the Child and Family Agency."

"Correct. We work closely with them. Regarding the case of the foundling girl, Tusla will provide the appropriate specialist child services. We, An Garda Siochana, will liaise closely with them and conduct the police inquiry."

"And in the meantime, the girl remains under my care in pre-foster care placement."

"Yes, Doctor Harrison. In **your** care, not under the care of Kevin Doherty."

"In my care? But located in Kevin Doherty's cottage?"

"I trust you can work with that. After all, it is what you proposed. Is it not?"

"Yes, indeed. But what has Afghanistan got to do with this?"

"Oh, that came up when we checked on your suitability to provide pre-foster care. You never told me you were famous."

"Famous? What do you mean?"

"Ah, I received some background information on your medical service in Afghanistan. Do you know what I am referring to?"

I was miffed at the police checking up on me. "I do not talk about Afghanistan."

Sergeant O'Dowd perused the computer monitor. "I see that you are highly regarded in treating stress disorders. And not just with combat troops. I see a report on your work with distressed children in a war zone."

"I do not talk about Afghanistan. I do not think about Afghanistan."

"Be that as it may, you appear to be perfectly qualified to treat the foundling girl."

Sergeant O'Dowd expected me to comment. I remained silent.

To break the silence, the sergeant added to his previous remark. "And we recommend that the girl remains in your care until other measures are implemented."

I was relieved to hear this. "Thank you, Sergeant. That is a prudent decision."

"It is more than simply prudent. We have a procedure for dealing with these situations. Where a child is rescued or found abandoned, we require a number of tests. Usually, these tests are conducted in a hospital in Dublin or other major centres. Where the subject child is in a remote location, it is unusual, but not unprecedented, to assign this task to a qualified doctor locally."

"And this is one of the 'unusual situations'? And Ardara is a 'remote location'?"

"Precisely. We recognize that it is not prudent to move the foundling at this time. Furthermore, we, An Garda Siochana and Tusla, are satisfied that you are suitably qualified. The required tests will be communicated to you, which you will duly conduct and report in the prescribed procedures."

I was familiar with the required procedures. I had encountered them in Afghanistan. Sergeant O'Dowd advised me that I would shortly receive an email from Tusla with instructions on the protocols and the subsequent online reporting.

*　　*　　*　　*　　*　　*　　*

On the next morning, when I entered Kevin's cottage, he was bursting to tell me the news. "Freddie, she spoke identifiable words. Can you believe that?"

I was excited at hearing this. "She did? That's great

news. And what words did she utter?"

"'Aw-aw' and 'aw-aw'."

My excitement vanished. These were not words, just uttered sounds. "So she said 'aw-aw'…"

"No, Fred. Not 'aw-aw'. It's 'aw-aw'."

I was becoming frustrated with Kevin. Was he playing a joke? "It either is, or it is not, 'aw-aw'. Which?"

"You're saying it wrong, Fred. Listen carefully. The first vowel is about a second long; the second one is slightly shorter. Also, the first vowel is pitched at a sustained C above Middle C. And the second vowel is sustained at the B flat, one tone lower. And that's just one word. There is a second word…"

"Hold on, Kevin. Let me understand. You are teaching her to say words consisting of vowels at specific pitches?" This was interesting, but not any more than the previous day's 'la-lahs'. It was not intelligent speech – just a parrot-like repetition of sounds.

"Wro-ong." Kevin uttered the word 'wrong' annoyingly, presumably pitched at C and B flat. "She taught me. And I understand the words."

This was beginning to irritate me. "Kevin, let's pretend,

for the moment, that I am immensely stupid. Now, tell me slowly and clearly what you are saying."

Kevin was unable to hide his excitement. Nevertheless, he slowed done to the speed of sense. "Yesterday, I was singing scales with the flotsam girl." Then he said aside to himself, "I must find a name for her," and continued speaking to me. "She talks in vowels at specific pitches. All her words are vowels, with the occasional 'kuh' and 'chuh' inserted as breaks. 'Sss' is used rarely. And it may not be part of a word at all."

This was an important breakthrough. If Kevin was correct, we had opened a means of intelligent communication – language. "Please continue." I was eager to hear more. I was not fully convinced. Kevin may have been exhibiting wishful thinking.

"She taught me the word for the soup I give her. And another word for the sardine sandwiches."

"Kevin, is this for real?"

"Let me prove it to you. I will demonstrate. You can judge from the evidence." The girl was looking at us with mild curiosity. She was sitting on a chair by the fire, blowing into a tin whistle. She formed prolonged notes and moved her fingers to alter the pitch. Through it all, she studied the dialogue between the two adult men. Kevin entered the kitchen. Moments later, he returned. He removed the tin whistle from the girl. He sounded one of the 'words' to her. The girl entered the kitchen. Kevin whispered to me, "She will fetch the bowl of soup." Sure enough, she returned with a bowl of soup. She returned to her chair and proceeded to drink from the bowl.

I was impressed, but not convinced. "How many items did she have to choose from in the kitchen?"

"Hah! You are not convinced. We will try it later. And she will choose from multiple items."

Some hours later, Kevin decided that it was time to conduct another demonstration. This time, he had me arrange objects on the kitchen counter – a plate containing a sardine sandwich, more soup but in a different bowl, a raw potato, an entire loaf of bread and the milk jug. He asked me to choose between the soup and the sandwich. I decided on the sandwich.

Back in the front room, the girl was scribbling on paper with a red pencil. She appeared to be in awe of the markings made by the pencil. Kevin took the pencil from her hand and said the word representing the sandwich. She entered the kitchen and reappeared with the sardine sandwich. She sat by the fire and ate it. I was convinced. Over the next few days, she would continue to demonstrate her ability to understand Kevin's words.

Kevin expanded on his understanding of language. He alluded to 'dentist talk' – speaking with your mouth wide open when a dental instrument is inserted in your mouth. He proceeded to speak to me exclusively in vowels. He asked me to pour him a cup of tea. I understood the request from his tone and body language. I complied. He played with me too. He rhymed some obvious words and then denied saying them. But he made his point.

"Kevin," I said. "I understand that one can communicate exclusively in vowels. But it is very limited."

"I agree. But consider the significance of pitch. High sounds – happy; higher sounds – jolly; low sounds – stern; lower – threatening; really low – hostile."

"Like Sergeants O'Dowd's gruff voice."

"Exactly. As to limitations, consider this. Over a span of four octaves, there are 48 notes. Only 48, right? That's the limit of the human voice. Yet, how many unique recognizable vocal melodies are there – past and present?"

"I don't know, Kevin. More than I can count."

"So, back to the girl. We don't know the extent of her language or her proficiency in it. But, here's what I **do** know – she is capable of learning. I will teach her. I have copies of all the school books from Infant Class to Sixth Class. And they are tastefully illustrated. Her lessons will begin tomorrow."

CHAPTER FIVE

LANTA: A DULCET NAME

I visited Kevin and the girl the following morning. It was a professional visit, of course, but heavily weighed with my desire to socialize with my reacquainted friend and his young dependent. When I entered the cottage, I was surprised, but pleased, to witness a new development. Kevin had rearranged the room like a school classroom. The 'pupil' sat at the desk while the 'teacher' stood in front conducting the 'class'. Kevin dressed for the part. He was attired in dress pants and a white shirt with a navy-blue tie. The girl's dress was a surprise. Knowing her aversion to wearing clothes, Kevin had fashioned a smock from a white dress shirt. It was loose-fitting and reached almost to her knees. The sleeves were rolled up to above her elbows. Her feet were bare as usual. I was pleased to see her properly clothed. Perceiving that the class was in session, and not wishing to interrupt the session, I tendered a quick greeting and left.

Throughout the day, I attended to my professional duties and returned to the cottage late in the afternoon. Kevin updated me on his work and gave an account of the child's development. He had established a routine for her – classes in the morning; activity in the afternoon, consisting of hiking or swimming; music and games in the evening. In between, there was time for eating and relaxing.

In a few days, the routine was firmly in place. The girl relished the order of the routine and she displayed an eagerness to learn. Kevin assigned study exercises for her, tasks that required her to execute on her own. During these periods, Kevin drove to the convenience store and obtained his daily groceries. He did a lot more than shop for groceries. He phoned around for school supplies and obtained them at prearranged roadside pickup. He engaged his father, the retired school inspector, to help. One day Padraig Doherty arrived with a carload of classroom materials – a chalkboard and easel, a globe of the world, and big glossy maps for the wall. And this was not all. While shopping in the convenience store, Kevin paused to read the notices on the community noticeboard. One posted note caught his attention – 'piano for sale, going cheap to a good home'. Kevin removed the note. Later, he phoned the contact number listed on it. And for €50, the seller delivered the piano to the cottage in his farm tractor. It took Kevin an entire day to tune the instrument. By the end of the week, Kevin and I revised our favourite ballads from former times. The girl was delighted with the music and insisted on joining the singing. In a short time, she had mastered *'My Lagan Love'* and *'Danny Boy'*. I was greatly taken by her sense of pitch and delicate expression. Her dulcet tones seemed to hang in the air after she finished.

Throughout this, I still had my professional obligation to perform. I consulted Kevin's daily journal and studied his account of the girl's progress. I elicited clarification on some of the entries. I was fully cognizant that, at some future point, the girl would be reunited with her family or kin. Until then, her emotional maturity and natural development would require her to socialize with other children and other people. It was only a matter of time until she would be separated from Kevin. I warned him not to get too attached – although a strong bond had already formed. Regardless of how events unfolded – uniting her with family and kin, or upon reaching a reasonable state of recovery from her trauma, or failing to recover fully – separation from Kevin was inevitable. My responsibility, and Kevin's, lay in providing her with an interim protective environment in which to recuperate.

I queried Kevin for clues on the child's identity. What information did he collect from her? He had learned a lot in ten days. One day while hiking on the headland, she stood looking westwards over the Atlantic swells. She chanted in long sorrowful tones. By then, the pair had developed sufficient language to communicate to a reasonable degree. Kevin asked her about her mournful song. She informed him that it was a song for her 'lost family'. She told him that they are somewhere out there (pointing to the ocean) 'in the water'. From Kevin's account, I deduced that the girl's family perished at sea and that she was now an orphaned survivor.

Kevin explained her aversion to clothing. She was unfamiliar with wool and cotton, and with many of our common fabrics. She accepted his cotton 'smock' but was frequently unclothed. Previously, in her former home, she wore 'Uwah skin'. Neither of us was familiar with 'Uwah skin'. But it suggested that her family were hunters. I made a mental note to convey this information to Sergeant O'Dowd.

I ventured that we might derive a clue from any skills she exhibited. According to Kevin, she loved to swim. He described their first visit to the sea together. "She was eager to descend the cliff. When she reached the shore, she recklessly plunged into the water. My heart skipped a beat. I feared that she might hit her head on a submerged rock. She swam like a fish. But then she ventured beyond the sandbar. This added to my distress. I shouted to her that this was not a safe place to swim due to the strong currents. She either did not hear, or she simply ignored me. I sat on the rocks anxiously watching her and praying for her safety. At one point, I believed that she was injured and in danger of drowning. She lay motionless, floating like a log. She was almost completely submerged. She appeared and disappeared between the swells of the waves. She looked lifeless, save for the brief times she turned her head to breathe. I was unable to help. I would have needed a boat to reach her. Suddenly, she sank beneath the surface. My heart sank. A few seconds later, she re-emerged. She waved at me and displayed a fish she held in her hand. She placed the fish in her mouth and swam back to me. Moments later, I hugged her in relief. She, on the other hand, was excited about her catch and was oblivious to the danger she had exposed herself to. The second time this happened, I noticed that she first viewed the sea from the cliff. She identified where she would swim. Then she rushed down the pathway to the shore and dived into the water, making for her predetermined location. I recognized that she had a talent for locating fish. And she was adept at catching them. Her skill was brilliant. She never went after fish. Instead, she floated around motionless where she expected the fish to swim. And she would snag one as they swam past. I had never seen that before. I didn't even know it was possible. Can you believe it? The fish swim up and, 'whoosh', she grabs it. Lord, Fred, I have trouble holding on to a dead fish, let alone attempting to grab on to a live one."

"Indeed, Kevin, that is a rare skill. But it is not unknown. I have heard of it but never witnessed it."

"Where could she have learned such a skill?"

I did not answer. This skill was one more piece to add to the girl's profile. We were one step closer to learning about where she came from. Could it be far-off Polynesia in the Pacific?

We probed her memory to ascertain a description of her home. Where was it? What were the living conditions? Did she come from a large family? As to where it was, she pointed to the ocean. That was not much help. We already knew she came ashore from the Atlantic. But from which land or region? As to her living conditions, she had not lived in a cottage such as Kevin's. She lived 'all over' wherever they went. This suggested a nomadic life. She indicated that her family was large. We attempted to estimate the number of family members. How many brothers and sisters? Her numbers ranged from six to one hundred. Math was not her strong subject. The vague number could have been another component of nomadic life. Family, as we know it, may have had a different meaning to her. Did she allude to extended family? Or kinsfolk? Or tribal family? Nomads often travel in small groups and assemble in greater numbers for certain events – weddings, festivals and migration. Could this have been the reason for the wide variance in describing the size of her family?

Since the time that she and Kevin accomplished a degree of communication – sometimes in her language and other times in English or a hybrid of both – we never learned her name. Surely, she knew her name. But acquiring her name proved to be an insurmountable challenge. I attended the session where Kevin tried to coax the information from her. She was unable to grasp the concept of a personal name.

As in all these sessions, Kevin played it like a guessing game. "Tell me, Girl-from-the-Atlantic, who am I?"

She pointed to him. "You're a Kevin." She pointed at me. "You're a Fred." And putting her hands on top of her head, "I'm a girl."

Kevin attempted another strategy. "When your mother called you, what did she say?"

"I can't say."

"You don't know?"

"Of course, I know. I can't say it."

"And why not? Is it private?"

"What's 'private'?" This conversation was a struggle.

Kevin exhibited patience. I had to admit that he was

good with children. "Tell me why you cannot say what your mother said, whenever she called you."

"Because she called me with her sound. I cannot say her sound. Only **she** can say her sound."

"Your mother called you using a unique sound?"

"What's 'unique'?"

He tried again. "What was special about the sound, so that you knew she was calling you?"

"Like how high the sound was."

"And from the pitch of her voice, you knew she was calling just you and no one else?"

"The pitch of her voice?" 'Pitch' was also a new word for her. "Yes."

"Let's say someone else called you. What would he say?"

"He would use **his** sound."

"The same sound as your mother used?"

"That's silly. Everyone used their own different sound. That's how I would know who was calling me."

"Ah, yes. Of course. Silly me."

"And she would say a different voice for everyone in the family. We all did. Everyone knew who was calling and who was being called when the right pitch was used. But no one used another person's call."

Kevin and I came to the same conclusion. The call identified the caller, not the person being called. And the pitch of the call targeted the person being called.

Kevin tried another approach. "Let's say I gave you a special name that no one else could have. Would you like that?"

"Yes. I would like that. And afterwards, you could give me another one. Could I have a new special name every day?"

"How about a special name that didn't change – one that stayed with you always."

At this, the girl laughed. "There's no such thing. If I change, the name changes. I could have a happy name. I could have an inside name. An outside name. But I don't want a sad name."

Kevin made one last attempt. "Tell me. What did you call your mother?"

The girl emitted a short high-pitched vowel.

"And what is that in English?"

"It's not in English. There is no English for that sound."

Kevin gave up. The girl did not have a name within our understanding of a personal name. And we did not understand personalized communication that employed pitch. Still, he was determined to give the girl a name. We could not continue to refer to her as 'the child', 'the waif' or 'jetsam'. He resumed talking to her. "We could call you 'Girl-from-the-Atlantic' because that's what you are." The girl understood 'Atlantic' to mean 'big water'. It was a description that identified the ocean, not its 'name'. Kevin's suggestion of a special name was acceptable to the girl. For as long as she remained here with Kevin, she would always be 'Girl-from-the-Atlantic'. But this name was applicable only in the context of their relationship and in this location. However. there was one snag with this name. It consisted of too many consonants. Kevin shortened it to 'Atlanta'. That was unmusical. Finally, they agreed upon 'Lanta' rendered in a sing-song fashion like a cuckoo call. The girl was delighted with her 'unique name'. She insisted that we repeat it numerous times. Kevin went to the piano and played *'The Cuckoo Song'* in G major. Whenever we reached the part that went *'Cuckoo, cuckoo'*, we altered the phrase to *'Lanta,*

Lanta'.

A week went by. I next visited at midday. Kevin and Lanta were about to proceed on a fishing venture. I joined them. I descended the cliff gingerly. When I reached the bottom, Lanta was already in the water. Kevin gestured to me to hurry and enter the boat. This was my surprising introduction to the boat.

"You have a boat? When did you get a boat?"

"Get in. And hurry. You don't want to miss the fishing experience."

It was a small wooden boat, able to accommodate four people. I entered the craft and realized that it was unstable. When I shifted my weight to sit securely, the boat rocked and I feared that it might capsize. Kevin appeared undeterred. He started the engine and we sailed through the calm inner waters of the inlet. The boat's wake churned white frothy bubbles, and the sea air filled my lungs and cleared my nose. Moments later, we reached Lanta. Thereupon, we bobbed together in the water, the floating girl and the buoyant craft side by side.

I asked Kevin about his new acquisition. "So, when did you get this thing?"

"It's great, isn't it? It's light enough for me to haul

ashore to above the high-tide point. And I am close enough to Lanta to keep her within reach. But it's not seaworthy. Oh, it's safe within the calm waters of the inlet, but I would not venture out beyond the headland, The whitecaps could swamp the boat."

I was puzzled about how he got the boat to his hidden cove. "Kevin, if the boat is not seaworthy, how on earth did you get it to your hidden cove? Surely, you didn't lower it down the cliff face? The only other access is past the neighbours' houses, a distance of a kilometre from the beach."

"Hah! That's where you're wrong. Do you know the wall at the roadside back at the waterfall?"

"That's two kilometres away."

"I had the supplier deliver the boat there, to the other side of the wall. Then we dragged the boat on rollers to the sand. When the spring tide came, I was able to float the boat to the inlet. It can float in 40 centimetres of water. It was only possible there during the spring high tide."

I considered all the changes that had occurred in Kevin's life in the one month since the arrival of Lanta. He was going out again, albeit with social distancing. He was singing again. And fishing again – fresh fish was added to his diet. And he was teaching again. At this rate, I was confident that he would soon return to society and undertake fulfilling employment. However, my primary focus was on Lanta's well-being. She was progressing well. If only we could reunite her with her home and kinsfolk, I was confident that Lanta would fully recover.

A week later, Kevin phoned. "Hello, Fred. I have learned something about Lanta that should interest you."

I was eager to hear more. "So, tell me. Does it pertain to her identity?"

"Yes. To her past life."

"That's great news. What is it?"

"Fred, I don't think it is all good news. Best if you come here so that I can better explain."

I immediately drove to the cottage. Upon entering, 20 minutes later, Kevin sat me down at the table, now a school desk. It was stacked with English readers, an atlas, and arithmetic books. He informed me that Lanta was preparing fish in the kitchen for the evening meal and was out of earshot. He sat beside me and indicated to the reading books.

"This book, Fred, is the reader for First Class. See, each page describes a trade or profession."

I knew that. I read the same book when I went to school. There is a page entitled 'The Farmer' with a smiling farmer driving a tractor past happy children and waving to us from the page. Then there is the page with a garda directing traffic and smiling at children crossing the road. A page on the railway porter. And the sea captain, the fireman and so on. I prompted Kevin to impart his urgent news. "And there is something from Lanta's home in this book?"

He did not give a direct answer. "Fred, think back. Do you remember what Lanta said – screamed, actually – when she encountered Sergeant O'Dowd?"

"Not exactly. Except that she screamed in fear when he approached."

"And that is what I thought at the time – just screams. But now that I understand her vocalizations, I know that she uttered precise words." Kevin opened the book at various pages. He pointed to the garda, the railway porter and the sea captain. "Lanta referred to these three men as 'Ah-aaah'," rendering the word as a cry. "What have these three men in common?" I was impatient for Kevin to get to the point. Seeing my agitation, he tendered the answer. "The uniform jacket. The word that she uttered translates as 'coat-man'."

"Lord, Kevin, this is significant."

"But, hold it. There is more."

With that, he opened a second book. This was the second-class reader. It contained stories and descriptions of other peoples and places. I remembered this book too. It had a page with a smiling Dutch girl picking tulips. And a page with a smiling Lapp boy with his reindeer. Kevin opened the book to his chosen spot marked with a bookmark. The page displayed a smiling Inuit hunter in his kayak paddling past a seal on an ice flow. The caption underneath identified the person as an Inuk, a member of an indigenous people of northern Canada and parts of Greenland and Alaska. And that his language is Inuktitut. Kevin revealed the reason for choosing this particular page.

"When I had Lanta read from this page, she pointed to the seal and said, 'Uwah'."

I immediately got the connection. Previously, Lanta revealed that her family wore 'Uwah skin'. I exclaimed excitedly, "Sealskin. They wore sealskin. Now, who wears sealskin?"

Kevin tapped his finger loudly on the open page. "The indigenous people of the Arctic."

"Lanta is from northern Canada."

"Somewhere in the Arctic regions of Canada or Greenland; maybe Lappland or Norway, Finland or Russia; it could also be the Aleutian region of Russia or Alaska."

"This is important progress. We must tell Sergeant O'Dowd and have him direct his inquiries to these countries, with particular attention to Canada."

"Not yet, Fred. Hold back. It's not all good news."

With this information, there was an increased chance of Lanta leaving us and returning to her home. This could only be good news, albeit unexpected at this juncture. Kevin could not regard it as anything else. I saw the unease in Kevin's face. I waited for him to impart the unwelcome part of his information. There was much more to learn. And it was disturbing.

After a pause, Kevin continued. "When Lanta recoiled from Sergeant O'Dowd in terror, she uttered another word. I just learned its meaning from Lanta this morning – 'Me-eater'. At first, I considered that I had misheard, or that Lanta had difficulty pronouncing 'meat-eater'. No. 'Me-eater' was her intended word and meaning. She was afraid of Sergeant O'Dowd because she believed that he would take her away to kill her and eat her."

I was dumbstruck at learning this. When I recovered, I challenged Kevin's interpretation of the girl's words. He was unyielding. He had checked and double-checked with her. The meaning was clear. After some deliberation, we arrived at three possible explanations: First, it was the product of a scary story, like the 'boogeyman' who dwells under a child's bed. Or a spin on 'don't talk to strangers' warning. Second, it was a fear with some basis but got distorted and larger-than-life in the child's imagination. I knew that children were abducted in some parts of the world and were enslaved. Some children served in armies as child soldiers. Did Lanta come from that situation? Third, it was literally true. Abducted children were eaten. True or not, it was real fear on Lanta's part. A disturbing element was the identity of the perpetrators – men wearing uniform jackets. I realized then that Lanta's trauma lay not solely in the storm she had survived, but was rooted primarily in her escape from a terrible experience in which she feared for her life.

It took me some time to recover. I glanced in at the girl busy in the kitchen with a spatula and frying pan. I considered what deep scars she was carrying. And I was amazed at how normal she appeared – working and singing as she performed her domestic tasks. Kevin boasted of her other skills – cutting and gutting fish; tying knots in strings to adjust the fit of her clothing. Although these tasks were new to her, she demonstrated a dexterity that could only have come from previously-learned skills.

After I left the cottage, I went directly to the garda station. I requested an urgent meeting with Sergeant O'Dowd. He complied. I revealed to him all that I had learned about the flotsam girl. O'Dowd was moved by my account. He questioned me intensely regarding the reliability of the girl's story. Could it have been wild imagination? Regardless, she exhibited fear of the 'coat-man' when the sergeant attempted to confront her. Real or imagined, the results were undeniable – the girl suffered great trauma. The sergeant decided that a visit by a child psychologist from Children's Services was due. I agreed. Actually, as per the protocols, the visit was overdue. Moreover, it was not the only thing that was overdue. I had not conducted the required blood tests on the girl. An attempt to draw blood would have been frightening to her. I delayed until an opportune time. Considering her fear of being eaten, I wondered when this might be.

CHAPTER SIX

VISITORS

Sergeant O'Dowd decided that it was time to pay another visit to Kevin's cottage. He needed to satisfy himself that the girl was being treated with care in a child-friendly environment. I warned him not to arrive unannounced dressed in his garda uniform.

"So, how should I dress?" he asked in his usual gruff voice.

"Are you ever out of uniform? You probably sleep in it."

He was miffed at my remark. "I have my Sunday suit. That should be acceptable."

"Don't you have something casual or sporty?"

He thought for a second. "I lounge about at home in a shirt and cardigan when I watch TV or potter about."

"Your TV lounging attire sounds right. Now, lighten up on the gruff voice – you sound like a garda."

This miffed him further. "I **am** a garda – a garda sergeant. I speak with an authoritative voice. It is appropriate, and it is expected."

"Well, turn it off when speaking to the flotsam girl – if

you ever get close enough."

"Ah, yes. If I get close. Have you any suggestions on that?"

"She is a child. Bring a gift that would appeal to her."

"I have no idea. What do you suggest?"

It was clear that the tough sergeant was not skilled in this area. "She likes school books. Oh, and food. All children like edible treats."

The sergeant brightened up. "Edible treats. That's a great idea. So, what does she like to eat?".

I had an image of Lanta in the kitchen. "She consumes eggs at times, but mostly fish, milk and potatoes."

"I could bring fish-and-chips."

At this, I laughed aloud. Sergeant O'Dowd was peeved once again. I had an idea and I prompted O'Dowd to make the suggestion. "The girl likes milk, rich creamy milk."

"Then how about ice cream? Children like ice cream."

"Excellent suggestion, Sergeant. I don't believe Lanta has ever tasted ice cream. This will be a special treat for her." So, it was settled. I would come to the cottage with Sergeant O'Dowd. And I would introduce him.

On the appointed day, I drove the sergeant to Maghera. En route, we stopped at the convenience store and purchased ice cream. I was prepared. I had a picnic cooler for the ice cream. Otherwise, it would have melted during the 15-minute journey.

Kevin had primed Lanta for our visit. She was going to meet a new friend. When the sergeant and I entered, Lanta hid in her room. However, she did not display any distress. Kevin coaxed her with the promise of a gift. He proffered her a sampling of ice cream on a spoon. She tasted it cautiously and she was immediately fascinated by the creamy texture and the pleasing taste of French vanilla. She ventured out to the front room where Sergeant O'Dowd presented her with an entire block of ice cream. Since it was beginning to melt, Kevin had the girl obtain bowls and spoons from the kitchen. The four of us sat around spooning ice cream into our mouths. Kevin warned the girl about the risk of 'ice cream headache' and insisted that she consumed a small spoonful at a time. Afterwards, she exhibited her literary skills by reading from the second-class reader. Her greatest display was in her singing. Kevin accompanied her on piano. She rendered her final song in her vowel language with the melody rising and falling strangely. It was clear to Sergeant O'Dowd that the girl was happy and was learning from Kevin's homeschooling. She certainly did not exhibit any troubling behaviour like on his previous visit. Afterwards, the girl whispered to Kevin. He informed us that we could stay for a meal, at Lanta's invitation. We agreed. The girl was eager to display her cooking skills too. She went to the kitchen to prepare the fish. It was going to be a fish dinner.

With Lanta busy in the kitchen, O'Dowd questioned Kevin on his recent findings. The sergeant sat at the table, now the school desk, where Kevin relayed the information he had previously conveyed to me. O'Dowd studied the relevant pages in the books and assessed their significance in light of what the girl expressed. He agreed with us that Lanta had experienced some ordeal, real or imagined, from 'men in coats'. He surmised that the child must have come from a region where people wear seal-skin clothes and where seals are common sights. He knew where he would direct his ensuing inquires on the girl's origin and home, and ultimately make contact with her next of kin. He would submit an inquiry to INTERPOL via International Liaison. A request to locate the family of a foundling child might not be treated with the same urgency as a criminal inquiry. The protocol is simple but slow. He decided on another quicker route – contact the Canadian Embassy for assistance. Canada provides an Emergency Watch and Control Centre for its citizens abroad. This is more likely to produce a speedy response.

It was now eight weeks since the girl was rescued. I was amazed at the progress she was making. Soon, she would be ready to venture out. To date, her only contact with people was with Kevin and me, and with Sergeant O'Dowd. Before I could take appropriate steps to address her deficiency in social interaction, I was presented with the answer. I was nervous about the upcoming test. It would either be very good and advance Lanta's social skills, or, it could be a failure and set her back. Sergeant O'Dowd explained that having filed his obligatory report, the girl was obliged to undergo a visit from Children's Services. A child psychologist was scheduled to conduct an official analysis of the girl's emotional and mental state. I agreed. I had no other option. However, I insisted that I, as the girl's doctor, be present at the psychological examination. Furthermore, Kevin, the closest thing to family in the girl's current situation, would be present also. Sergeant O'Dowd agreed. He realized that he, too, had no other option. He was not prepared to risk a complaint from the patient's family doctor.

On the appointed day, we arrived at the cottage, Sergeant O'Dowd, Doctor Kathleen McBrearty and I.

O'Dowd and McBrearty travelled in a garda car; I proceeded them to forewarn Kevin. I had performed my due diligence in researching the reputation and qualifications of Doctor Kathleen McBrearty – Doctor of Psychological Science (DPsychSc) in Clinical Psychology. She was employed by Tusla, the Child and Family Agency of the Department of Children, Equality, Disability, Integration and Youth. Tusla provides specialist services for separated children seeking asylum. Children are referred by the Garda National Immigration Bureau. Sergeant O'Dowd's report would have been forwarded as a matter of course. The majority of children are initially accommodated in one of the intake units as either a 'pre-reunification with their family placement', or as a 'pre-foster care placement'. Unaccompanied children under 12 years of age are placed with a foster family on arrival. Children are received into care by the Agency, either on a voluntary basis or through a court order under the Child Care Act 1991. Some children are placed into care while family tracing is being facilitated.

Doctor McBrearty's assessment and recommendations would determine if, or for what period, Lanta could remain with Kevin. Since we did not know Lanta's age with certainty, she could be treated either as a child under 12 or over 12. This was a pivotal point in determining how and where she might be placed by Tusla.

Sergeant O'Dowd remembered to dress in civilian clothes. He also remembered to stop at the convenience store to purchase ice cream. Doctor McBrearty was in her professional attire – a dark-blue skirt and white blouse. Her black medium-heeled shoes were town shoes, suitable for rural visits, but unsuited to the rough terrain of Knockfola headland. Nevertheless, she stepped lightly and radiated a cheerful disposition. I could see how she would be accepted warmly by children. Inside the cottage we re-enacted the previous ritual – Lanta hid in her room, Kevin coaxed her with ice cream and she overcame her shyness to join us in consuming fast-melting ice cream.

This was Lanta's first experience with an adult female since her arrival. She gazed at the newcomer's strange attire. She was particularly curious about Doctor McBrearty's shoes. She whispered to Kevin to enquire if her feet were 'that shape'. We overheard her question and smiled, even Doctor McBrearty smiled. The pleasing snack of ice cream and Lanta's humorous question opened an opportunity for Doctor McBrearty to speak.

"I'm Doctor McBrearty. But my real name is Kathleen McBrearty. People who like me, call me 'Kay'. You can call me Kay.

Lanta nodded in understanding. She was not sure if such a harsh consonant was suitable for a name.

Kay McBrearty continued. "And what is your name?"

Lanta replied in her sing-song fashion, "Lanta."

"Well, Lanta, I am pleased to…"

"My name is 'Lanta'," articulating it musically. "It is not 'Lanta'," rendered in monotone.

Kay was confused. She did not perceive the difference.

Kevin came to her rescue. "Her name is 'Lanta' rendered musically." Kevin repeated her name to demonstrate. "Lan-ta."

The doctor tried again. It was at this point that we realized that she was tone-deaf. She was unable to render the name correctly. "Well, Lanta, I am pleased to meet you."

Kevin chuckled aloud. I stifled a laugh. Sergeant O'Dowd tried to suppress a snicker. He pretended to cough. Kay asked us what was so funny.

Kevin explained. "You sound just like an English person trying to pronounce an Irish name."

"That bad, is it?" She too laughed. She composed herself and continued to speak with the girl. "So, tell me. How old are you?"

To which Lanta answered, "I'm not old. **You** are old." More smiles and chuckles all around.

Kay made a few futile attempts to ascertain the girl's age. Finally, she addressed us. "Do we know her age?"

I answered. "I'm afraid not. I estimate 12."

"Yes. You are probably right."

"Is it important?"

"I'm afraid so. We treat cases differently depending on the age of the child – 12 and over, or, under 12."

During the meeting, Lanta demonstrated her reading skills and her singing. Kay was impressed that the girl had learned so much in two months. She questioned Kevin. "You say that she had no knowledge of English when you first found her?"

"No English and no Irish. At first, I learned a few words in her language and it took off from there. Now we communicate in a combination of both languages."

"What? You understand her native language. So, what

is it?"

"I don't speak her language in the sense that I know it. Some things are expressed differently – sometimes better in English, and at other times in song. Oh, her language is based on musical tones and consists entirely of vowels. We sing when we communicate."

"And there is such a language?"

"I never learned a language like this. But there are some almost-extinct languages that are based on sung vowels. I read that once, but I cannot remember where. If you are asking me if I can identify her native language, the answer is 'No'."

"One other thing. That's an unusual smock she is wearing. It looks like an altered man's shirt."

"So it is. We live in a remote cottage by the sea and it is summer. The smock is like beachwear or sundress. If she were to socialize, I would provide her with suitable alternative clothing."

"Do I understand that the girl does not socialize outside of this group?" She indicated to Kevin and me.

I provided the answer, notwithstanding that the question was directed at Kevin. "I am working on introducing Lanta to society. She has already made great progress in the time she has been with us. Sergeant O'Dowd can attest to that."

The sergeant interjected. "That's right. I can confirm that. Spectacular progress."

Kay continued to grill me. "You have experience in this field?"

"I worked as a medical officer in the British Army serving in Afghanistan. I am familiar with PTSD."

"You are familiar with Post Traumatic Stress Disorder?"

"Damn right I am – with its symptoms and treatment. It was a priority for us in active duty in a war zone. And God knows, we treated a lot of it in Afghanistan and afterwards upon returning home."

Kay nodded at this. I hope she felt chastened by my response to her inappropriate questioning of my medical skills.

I resumed speaking. "Today, Lanta widened her social circle by one. In the upcoming days, I will introduce her to an ever-widening circle until she is comfortable in a populated setting. That would include playing, shopping and interacting with children her age."

"I see. Well, I think I am done here." She addressed Lanta. "Lanta, it was a pleasure meeting you. I hope to see you soon again."

When the sergeant and the psychologist departed, Kevin and I devised a plan to retain temporary custody of the child until she would be reunited with her family. If Tusla decided that Lanta could remain with Kevin, no action was required. On the other hand, if living with Kevin was deemed unsuitable, which was likely, the girl would be placed in pre-foster care placement. We considered Kevin's parents as suitable candidates to provide pre-foster care. Two questions arose. Would the Doherty family in Inver be deemed suitable by Tusla? And would Padraig and Maura Doherty be willing to accommodate the girl in temporary placement – provided that the girl herself would be willing to live with them? Kevin did not intend to have the girl move in with his parents. Inver is a 30-minute drive from Maghera. Lanta could reside officially in Inver and, in reality, continue to live with Kevin. We had a Plan 'A', and a Plan 'B' if it was acceptable. But we did not have a Plan 'C'.

CHAPTER SEVEN

AN OUTING

Kevin telephoned his parents. "Hello, Da. Is that you?"

"Kevin?" Padraig Doherty removed the phone from his ear but was still audible to Kevin. "Maura, Kevin is on the phone." He resumed talking to Kevin. "So, how did the school supplies work out? Are you doing tutoring or something?"

"Yeah. I suppose I am."

"And how many pupils do you have?"

"One."

"Just the one? Ah, here's your Ma on the other line."

Maura Doherty spoke on the extension line. "Hello, Kevin. It's nice to hear from you. How are you keeping?"

Kevin was impatient to get to the purpose of his phone call. "I'm great. Fred Harrison is here with me. We are all doing well. Listen. I want to put something to you."

"Oh, yeah?" A request from a son recovering from trauma could be challenging. Maura braced herself.

"There's a young girl I'd like you to meet…"

"What? You have a girlfriend?"

"No Ma. She's living with me and…"

"You are living with a girl. Is that wise?"

"Listen Ma. Let me finish. I have a girl living with me. She is suffering from trauma. Fred – Doctor Harrison, you know – is treating her."

"That's very strange. Why is she living with you?"

"It is only until she is reunited with her family. Her immediate family may have perished. We don't know. We have not made contact with her kin yet. The guards are working on it. She is living here because she is afraid of strangers, and that's everyone besides Fred and me. Lord knows, I know exactly how she feels. Fred says that she is improving and that she needs to socialize with new people at this time."

"And you want us to socialize with her?"

"Well, yes. Someone sympathetic to her condition."

"What age is she – this disturbed girl?"

"We don't know. The girl does not know. We estimate that she is 12 years of age."

"What? Do you mean to say that you are living with a

12-year-old girl out there in the wilds?"

"The cliffs of Maghera, Ma. It is a haven for her. And she loves the sea."

"This is all very strange. But I suppose we could come for a visit and see how you are doing – both of you."

"Or we could come to visit you in Inver. Lanta – that's her name – has not ventured outside the cottage since I found her washed up by the sea…"

"Washed up by the sea? Lord, have mercy."

"Yes, Ma. I found her in the big cave after that fierce storm back in April. Since then, she has not ventured outside the cottage except to spend time by the shore below the cliff."

"Lord, Kevin, I don't know what to say."

"Fred believes that it is time to introduce her to people as part of her treatment. But this is all very secretive. We need to protect her from prying neighbours and inquisitive reporters. Unwanted social contact might retard her recovery and set her back. She is emotionally delicate."

"All right. I suppose she could visit us in Inver. It's a quiet spot, so there's no need to worry about nosy people."

"Oh, Ma. One thing more. She has no clothes."

"What do you mean? She runs around naked all the time?"

"No. She runs barefooted. The soles of her feet slap like shoe leather when she walks. She will only wear things that are loose and flowing – nothing tight or fitted. So, for clothing, she wears my shirts as dresses and smocks. She has taken to adorning them with leather boot thongs to which she has attached shiny stuff like bottle caps. And she applies knots to the garments to adjust the fit and length. Because of her fear of people, I can't take her shopping for clothes. And I don't know what to get for her. Could you help out with this?"

"A 12-year-old girl, you say? I'll come up with something."

"Good. I'll phone you later when we decide on which day to visit."

Upon terminating the call, I asked Kevin, "You did not bring up the matter of possible pre-foster care?"

"No. That would have been too much to present at one time. I'll broach that subject when we visit Inver. Let's see if the girl will take to Ma and Da, and vice-versa, and hope it goes well."

Later, in the afternoon, we ventured away from the cottage for the first time. Previously, Lanta had always been within sight of the house and within earshot of the sea. On this day we introduced Lanta to a short car trip. As usual, when he presented something new or strange, Kevin played it like a game. I played along. Kevin sat in the driver's seat. Lanta and I occupied the rear seat. Kevin put the car in motion and immediately brought it to an abrupt stop.

Kevin exclaimed in mock annoyance, "There's something wrong with the car. It won't go." He looked back at us in the rear seat and said, "Ah, that's the reason. The seatbelts. The car won't go until the seatbelts are attached."

Knowing her resistance to tight clothing, the seatbelt could be a challenge. I assisted Lanta in securing her belt and fastened mine, remarking how easy it was. Thus satisfied, Kevin proceeded down the laneway. The girl was uncomfortable in the unfamiliar constraint of the seatbelt. She tugged at it in irritation. Fortunately, her curiosity outweighed her discomfort and she gazed excitedly out the window at the passing landscape. Kevin turned right at the end of the laneway and proceeded west on the narrow coast road devoid of markings and signage.

We had gone less than a hundred metres when Lanta cried out. "Stop! Stop!"

Kevin brought the car to a halt. I checked to see if the seatbelt was irritating the girl. I asked what the problem was, fearful that this outing may have been premature.

"I can't hear the Atlantic," she exclaimed in alarm.

I realized then, that since arriving at Kevin's cottage, Lanta had never been out of earshot of the ocean. Kevin turned off the engine. We opened the doors. We could hear the crashing of the waves in the distance.

Kevin calmed the girl. "See. We are travelling along the headland. Look up there. That's where you frequently walk: The Atlantic is just over there, below the cliff."

The girl listened to the familiar sound of the sea and breathed in the salty sea air. She was relieved at this. We continued on our journey with the windows open wide. As we proceeded slowly on the isolated road, Lanta experienced a sense of freedom as the wind blew her hair. Satisfied that the ocean was close by, she settled into enjoying the experience. After five minutes, Kevin executed an audacious three-point turn on the narrow road at the Owenwee River Waterfalls. I exited the car to view his wheels and direct his manoeuvre. We returned to the cottage. The girl was exhilarated by the experience. We promised to repeat the adventure on the following day, and extend the journey even farther.

On the next day, we embarked on a second outing. This time we passed the Owenwee River Waterfalls and proceeded to a T-junction. Here, we encountered the first road sign since leaving the cottage – Left to Ardara; Right to Port and Carrick. Kevin turned right. The road was just as narrow as before. But the coastal heath was less intrusive this far inland. A strip of stubby grass grew along the centre line of the road. Notwithstanding, the area was populated. We viewed neatly whitewashed houses at intervals. At one point we met a postal van. The driver pulled alongside the entrance of a roadside house to permit us to pass. The uniformed driver – a 'man in a coat' – waved to us. Lanta bent down to hide from him. Once passed, she resumed her normal position. Kevin drove in the direction of Carrick until he reached Meenaneary, where he took a right fork on the R230 towards the ocean.

We encountered the sea once more at the village of Glencolmcille. Lanta regarded the collection of houses with interest. People walked about and seemed not to notice us in the car. Lanta felt secure in her bubble. A group of excited children ran out of the village school. It was the end of the school day and the start of the summer holidays. Lanta was fascinated by their joyous shouting and colourful clothes. She quizzed us on who the people were, what they were doing and why they dressed in colourful clothes. Lanta's clothes were exclusively fashioned from Kevin's white shirts. It struck me that, by comparison to the school children, she and Kevin were always outfitted in plain colours. I dressed in sober attire in keeping with my professional status. Even the sergeant, when not in uniform, dressed drably. And the psychologist, who visited once, was lacking in cheery colours. Kevin promised to obtain colourful clothes for the girl.

We drove back to the cottage without incident. I was pleased with the excursion. Lanta displayed natural childish curiosity. Apart from the brief incident when she felt obliged to hide from the postman – the man in a coat – the outing was an overall positive experience for her. She was ready for the next trip. That would be a half-hour drive to Inver, to meet new people face to face.

Kevin made arrangements with his parents. We waited until after the weekend. Coastal villages and beach areas attract visitors on weekends. So, we travelled to Inver on the following Monday. At first, I was concerned that Lanta would long for the proximity of the sea. I need not have worried. We crossed the

Bluestack Mountains to the south side of the headland on the N56. Because of the elevation of the road, the ocean was visible most of the time.

Inver is a scattered village. Twenty houses line the seafront. Another thirty or so stretch inland from the shore. Eany Water dissects the seaside strand of Salthill Bay Beach. The village of Inver is at the river mouth ('inver' means 'river mouth'). And the Doherty house and pub are located at the seashore where the river enters the bay.

The Doherty house is a solid two-story structure of limestone with a slate roof. It is aptly suited to its location close to the seashore. It has two front doors, side by side. The oak door affords entrance to the private dwelling; the ornate wood-and-glass door serves as the entrance to the pub. Upon entering the house, Padraig welcomed us warmly. As is his custom, he greeted us in Irish. Lanta made the required polite response, albeit shyly. Maura fussed over us and offered lemonade to Lanta. The girl declined the drink. Kevin informed his mother that Lanta has a limited diet and to substitute milk. This was acceptable.

Lanta sat quietly, sipping warm milk. She glanced around at the strange, yet wonderful, surroundings. She was seated in a large chair, a plush soft chair, with colourful cushions and lace covers on the armrests. The ticking clock on the mantle arrested her attention. A pendulum swung to and fro with every loud tick. She was suddenly surprised when the clock unexpectedly struck a note at the quarter-hour. She was amused by the musical clock that 'sang' the time. She cast her eyes around the walls. There were pictures high up and low down; pictures of people, pictures of animals and pictures of nothing at all except delightful bright colours. But one object, in particular, was a treasure trove – the glass-fronted dresser. She was fascinated by it. It displayed delicate pale-blue porcelain items – plates, cups, saucers, bowls and things she had never seen before. She continued to survey the room. She laughed audibly upon seeing flowers growing inside the house in shiny brass pots. She wondered how different this house was from Kevin's cottage on the cliff.

Padraig reverted to speaking in English and asked about my medical practice in Ardara. Meanwhile, Maura took Lanta to an adjoining room with Kevin in tow. She had laid out an array of clothing deemed appropriate for a 12-year-old girl. Lanta was greatly taken by a sundress in daffodil yellow. Within minutes, Maura had removed the girl's shapeless white smock and replaced it with the sundress. She tut-tutted in Kevin's direction at the absence of underwear and had the girl wear cotton hipster briefs with a floral pattern. She and Lanta viewed the result in a full-length mirror. Both were delighted at the transformation.

"Turn around and let me look at you," Maura said admiringly. "And how about a matching yellow bow for your hair?"

Lanta was uncomfortable wearing the bow. It tugged at her hair. She preferred her straight black hair to fall naturally. Having dispensed with the need for hair adornment, Maura turned her attention to the girl's feet.

"My, my. These are like the Conneely kids' feet – wide at the toes."

From the doorway, Kevin asked, "And what's peculiar about the Conneely feet?"

"The Conneely children don't like to wear shoes. They are barefooted most of the time. And when they wear boots, they choose large sizes that can be flung off quickly. I don't know if they have wide toes due to going barefoot, or if they choose to go barefoot because of the discomfort of shoes."

"I never noticed."

"Don't you remember, Kevin, when you first went dancing, that the Conneely girls never wore stiletto shoes with narrow toes?"

"Well, yes. But I thought it was their choice to wear Irish dancing style shoes."

"No, it wasn't. They needed wide-fitting shoes. And now, here is Lanta with the same feet."

"I don't believe she has ever worn shoes."

"That could account for it. Like the Conneelys, all right."

Later, we ate a meal of fish. Fish was in season and was freshly caught. Lanta, in her daffodil-coloured sundress, ate her fish and potatoes and drank her milk. The visit was going well. For a while, she fidgeted and tugged at the clothing at her waist. I could see that the elastic of her unfamiliar underwear was irritating her. Kevin took her aside and returned moments later with a floral-patterned handkerchief protruding from his pants pocket.

We went walking along the shore in the afternoon. There is a secluded patch of sand around the curve of the shore facing the old graveyard. It is where Kevin and I once went swimming. We encountered Carmel Conneely sitting on a rock while she kept an eye on her younger siblings playing in the water. The children were swimming naked, as I once did at this same secluded spot. At Maura's prompting, Lanta slipped out of her yellow dress and plunged into the water. The children were playing a racing game, swimming around a floating beachball. In the water, Lanta was less shy. She kept a distance from the other children and refrained from speaking to them. But she understood the 'rules' of the game and joined them in their swimming antics. The Conneelys are all great swimmers. But on this occasion, Lanta easily outswam them in the game.

Carmel addressed Maura. "Your granddaughter is a fine swimmer. Is she a member of a swim team?"

"I don't think she is a member of anything. But I agree, she knows how to swim."

The Conneely children left the water. They tossed the ball around on the beach so that they could run and dry off. Lanta remained in the water, staying submerged for long periods and exploring the area. Kevin gestured to Lanta to come ashore. She joined us. She objected to being dried by a towel provided by Carmel. Instead, she wore it like a cloak and thus we walked back to the Doherty house.

Back in the house, Lanta donned her yellow dress once more. Maura presented her with additional clothing – a blue V-neck cardigan and skirt, 'suitable for school'. Footwear was a challenge. She tried several open-toed sandals from her collection. She settled on a pair, a very old worn pair. From this, she determined a suitable shape and size for Lanta and promised to obtain new shoes for her at a future visit, perhaps lace-up wide-toed trainers.

It was time to broach the subject of fostering. When we were assembled, Kevin asked his parents to consider a proposal concerning Lanta. They looked at him inquiringly and waited in anticipation. Instead of coming to the point, Kevin asked me to present his request. This came without warning. I was not prepared for a professional presentation.

Leaving me to speak on his behalf and present his delicate request, Kevin took Lanta into the pub saloon and proceeded to play the piano. He and Lanta lilted a collection of their familiar melodies. The pub was empty of patrons except for a solitary drinker at the bar whose focus was entirely on his glass of stout. Eamon, the barman and Maura's brother, was stacking shelves and polishing glasses and seemed oblivious to the other occupants in the bar. The drinker rapped the counter with his knuckles to arrest Eamon's attention and have him provide another pint. Kevin and Lanta were on the far side of the room which, in this situation, was far away.

I spoke to Padraig and Maura. They were attentive.

They did not interpose. Had it been Kevin, they would have interrupted frequently. Now I understood why Kevin entrusted the presentation to me. I started with the account of Kevin rescuing the girl from the sea after a fierce storm. At the time, Kevin was suffering from stress disorder. The rescued girl also displayed similar symptoms. Both exhibited fear of social contact and relationships. They shunned public places and were liable to experience panic attacks when people were present. But strangely, they recognized a kinship in their shared phobia and reciprocated in helping each other. As a result, both made rehabilitating progress. I made it clear to Padraig and Maura that both patients remained in a delicate state, notwithstanding the significant progress in their recovery. An additional traumatic event could cause serious relapse in both of them and render a worse state than hitherto. In the event that the girl was not reunited with her family or kinsfolk, she would be taken by Tusla's Children's Services. In my opinion, the girl was not yet ready to socialize. She had a deep fear of 'men in coats'. If she was taken by Tusla, she would undoubtedly suffer distress. I gave an account of the events since the storm – the unsettling encounter with the uniformed Sergeant O'Dowd, the worrisome visit by the Tusla psychologist. My greatest fear was that both Kevin and Lanta could be distressed to breaking point if she were forcibly removed from his care. I ended with the suggestion that

Padraig and Maura might consider adoption.

Padraig summarized with questions. "This foundling girl is expected to be reunited with her family?"

"Yes. Sooner or later. We are optimistic."

"But if she is not reunited soon, she will be taken into foster care and placed with unfamiliar people. And this could be stressful for her – possibly triggering a breakdown."

"Stressful, without a doubt. Suicide is a risk. Irrespective, it would be detrimental to her mental health and well-being."

"Unless she was placed with Kevin. And you tell me that Kevin may not qualify as a suitable foster parent. So, if I understand you correctly, if Maura and I were accepted as foster parents, we would be proxies for Kevin. The girl would continue to reside with Kevin but officially here with us."

"Initially. In a short time, within a year I expect, both Kevin and the girl will have recovered sufficiently to enjoy 'normal' lives. And, in the interim, Lanta would be eased into living with you full-time in Inver."

"...where she would interact with village life, play with children her age, go to the local school, etc., etc."

"And at no time would Kevin be out of the picture. He is only a half-hour drive away."

Maura was silent throughout. Now she spoke. "Lord, Padraig, what's there to think about? The wee girl needs a loving environment. We can give that to her. It would be such a joy for us too."

"Until she is reunited with her family," Padraig responded. "But yes, I agree. Whether it is for a short time or an extended time, let's help out."

With this agreed upon, I planned to report to Sergeant O'Dowd and initiate a foster-parent application with Tusla for Padraig and Maura Doherty.

On the drive back to Maghera, we were filled with optimism. Lanta's future happiness was safeguarded.

CHAPTER EIGHT

CANADIAN, EH?

After the visit to Inver, Lanta was more outgoing. She still avoided people, but she ventured farther from the cottage in her solitary walks – a yellow-clad girl wandering the coastal cliffs and frolicking naked in the seawater below. I was busy too – updating Sergeant O'Dowd on the girl's improving health and instigating the process of having Padraig and Maura Doherty accepted as foster parents. The sergeant, in turn, had interesting news to report. The Canadian Embassy requested an interview with Lanta to determine if she was a Canadian citizen in need of assistance.

Canadian officials work closely with local authorities to advocate for the safety and well-being of Canadian children outside Canada. They are particularly concerned where the child is a victim of abduction, sexual assault, neglect, physical violence or abuse. I welcomed the Canadian attention. I considered that Lanta's distress resulted from some trauma other than being lost at sea. There was some ordeal in her past associated with 'men in coats'. Could she have experienced a violent or abusive situation? Perhaps even an abduction? Kevin may have rescued her from a lot more than a turbulent sea. So, I instructed the sergeant to advise the Canadians of the girl's fragile state and to conduct the interview delicately. The sergeant knew, from his personal experience, what protocols to observe in dealing with the child.

Summer holidays bring visitors to the sea. On my next visit to the cottage, I slowed my car when passing the access pathway to Maghera Beach. There was a rental car parked at the roadside. I was curious about the non-local visitors. Inquisitive Mrs Bonner (not that I too was nosy) was standing close by and looking towards the beach. I stopped alongside. Before I spoke, Mrs Bonner volunteered the information I sought.

"They're French, those ones." She pointed to the rental car. "Two of them, come all the way from France just to walk on the beach and go to the caves. Would you believe that? And sure, have they no beaches nor caves in France at all? And they come all the way here?"

"Well, Mrs Bonner, that shows you how renowned this place is."

Her children, Brendan and Babs, and one other boy joined her. Brendan spoke on behalf of the trio. "We follied them. They went into the big cave. But we came back afore they seen us."

Mrs Bonner continued. "Lord, this place can't stand the crowds. Just yesterday I seen five people on the strand. Five at the one time. That's how crowded it's getting around here."

I suppressed a smile. But for the life of me, I could not remember seeing anyone on the beach at any time. There is a partial view of the beach from Kevin's cottage, but not of the sheltered area furthest from the open ocean. That is the area accessible by a pathway from the road and where there is minimal risk of currents and undertows. That might explain why I never noticed the 'crowds' on the beach. Lanta, when she went swimming, avoided the sandy inshore beach. She favoured the seclusion of the rocky cove beneath the cliffs.

I was curious about the boy. I did not recognize him. "I see that it's getting crowded in your house too, Mrs Bonner. Is this an addition to your clan?"

The woman pointed to the boy. "Oh, this is Declan. He's my brother Michael's boy. He drives a bus in Dublin, y'know. Michael does, not the cub."

"Up here on his summer holidays?" I asked.

"Oh, indeed. Sure, the childer love the seaside, y'know."

"Indeed, they do, Mrs Bonner. Well, I'm off."

"Still treating the quare Doherty fellah?"

I drove out of earshot and pretended not to hear her parting question. However, Mrs Bonner alerted me to the increased human activity in the area. If Lanta was to remain hidden, we would need to exercise greater caution than heretofore.

My concern proved to be prophetic. On the following morning, as per the daily routine, Brendan and Babs delivered the milk and eggs to the gatepost at Kevin's laneway. But on this occasion, Declan accompanied them. Whether it was a dare or the boldness of the city boy, they ventured closer to the cottage than the set limit of the gatepost. Lanta was on the cliffside of the cottage at the time, twirling her dress to catch the breeze. The three children glimpsed the girl in the yellow sundress. They shrieked in surprise and ran back towards the lane. Lanta heard the cry. She bolted for the security of the cottage. Babs, the youngest child, cried to her brother to wait for her, fearful that she would be left behind at 'mad Doherty's place'. Brendan grabbed her wrist and pulled her. At that instant, he saw the strange girl enter the cottage. The entire incident occurred within a few seconds. But Lanta had been spotted by the Bonner children. And with Mrs Bonner's excellent broadcasting service, the entire neighbourhood would know within a few hours that there was a girl in the 'mad Doherty's house'.

Kevin phoned me regarding the incident. He was worried that it would bring unwelcome attention with detrimental results. I drove to Maghera to mitigate the effects. Getting Mrs Bonner's attention was easy. I simply stopped the car and she came out to investigate.

"Ah, Doctor Harrison? You're spending a lot of your time out here these days."

"Hello, Mrs Bonner. Any crowds today?"

"No, not today."

"No French visitors, or other strangers?"

"You know, it's funny you say that. I hear tell that there is a wee cutty up there in Doherty's cottage."

"Is that a fact? And why do you say that?"

She lowered her voice and leaned in closer. "The childer seen her this morning – Declan and my own two."

"Declan? Your nephew from Dublin?"

"Aye, him."

"Well, you know, even the Dohertys have kin. Perhaps Kevin Doherty has a relative visiting. It is the summer holidays after all."

"I don't know. Kevin Doherty has no childer. There's none in Inver that I know of. But then, his sister Nora is married with childer somewhere down the country. Maybe it's one of hers."

"Well, there you are, Mrs Bonner. It's as you say – it's the summer holidays and children love the seaside." I drove off before she could speculate any further. However, the secret was out – there was a young girl in the cottage with Kevin Doherty. But if the girl was perceived as visiting kin, there was nothing strange to report. I hoped that this would quell unwanted disturbing rumours. In time, the true nature of the girl would be discovered. I hoped that by then, her situation would be resolved.

The day of the Canadian Embassy's official visit arrived. It was conducted with correct protocols. The Canadian official worked with An Garda Siochana, in this case with Sergeant O'Dowd. I, as the girl's family doctor, was present at the interview. And Kevin Doherty, of course. The Canadian official, Brian McCann, was young and cheerful. He had been briefed on the circumstances of the girl's plight from the time she was cast ashore by the storm at Maghera to her current state of rehabilitation. He assured us that he was experienced in dealing with similar cases in working with refugee children and asylum seekers.

Brian McCann is Canadian-born. His father was an RUC police officer who emigrated to Canada during the troubles and joined the Peel Regional Police in Ontario. I was worried that the visiting official would be a 'suit' or a 'man in a coat'. This was not the case. Brian McCann was dressed in tan loafers, grey cargo pants with big pockets, a red checked shirt and a dark-green sweater. He was far from colour-coordinated. And he had tussled brown hair. Had I met him on a rural walk, I would have considered him appropriately attired. Instead of a briefcase, he carried a small wicker basket. He had been alerted to bring a gift, so I assumed that it was in the basket. I viewed the basket with interest. This Canadian guest was expected, but not in such casual clothing.

He introduced himself. "Brian McCann, from the Canadian Consular Services. I believe you are expecting me." He smiled effortlessly as he spoke. And the smile lingered. I wondered if the smile was his natural expression of repose. He continued. "Oh, don't worry about the McCann part. I get 'McCann', 'McGinn', 'McGann' and whatnot. But everyone gets it right with 'Brian'."

It was clear that the interview would be informal. I was relieved. Brian entered the front room as if he were completely familiar with it. He placed his wicker basket on the table and flipped open the lid. He remained standing, or more correctly, he moved about as he spoke. I observed his strategy. He was forewarned that he would be meeting a distressed child who shied away from strangers. His manner was relaxed and homely. Furthermore, he searched for Lanta with his eyes as he glanced around. He deduced correctly, that she was hiding within earshot. Perhaps even stealing a peek at him from a secure place. The bedroom with the half-opened door registered with him. Brian reamed off his introduction as to the purpose of his visit – the legalese preamble to a formal meeting. While speaking, he drew three coloured balls from a pocket and juggled them in the air with as much nonchalance as one might idly rub one's nose. Lanta, from the concealment of the bedroom, followed his movements with her eyes. As Brian moved around the room, she came through the bedroom doorway to keep him in her sight. Brian appeared not to notice. He continued with his preamble speech. He placed the juggling balls back in his pocket and drew out a sock. This he placed over one hand and engaged the sock puppet to deliver the conclusion of his introduction. I did not know whether to laugh or applaud. I did neither. Sergeant O'Dowd was puzzled by the performance. This was not how a government representative was expected to behave. Kevin, on the other hand, was right in step with the Canadian and played along like Abbot and Costello.

Brian drew a large book from the basket and placed it on the table. I recognized the title – Canadian Geographic. It is a magazine published by the Royal Canadian Geographical Society. The magazine is noted for its articles on physical, political and environmental geography. It is lavishly illustrated with photographs and maps, and it covers subjects such as acid rain, clear-cut logging, vanishing wetlands and other environmental issues. Brian explained, and sometimes via the sock puppet, that the interview would be recorded and that he would take pictures to assist in repatriating the girl to her next of kin. A recording of the girl's voice and picture images were necessary. We approved. And further, he requested a DNA sample. I agreed to obtain a sample at the first opportunity.

I leaned over to Sergeant O'Dowd and whispered, "Did you get the result of the test on the DNA sample I provided to you?"

He whispered back. "Ah, yes. And that's another matter we need to address. I just heard back. The test failed. The sample was too contaminated to provide an accurate result."

"Contaminated? How was it contaminated?"

"I don't know if was contaminated here, or from your plastic pouch, or if the lab messed up. All I know is that the sample was contaminated to the point of rendering it defective. Right now, we require another sample – a clean uncontaminated sample."

I resolved to be extra careful in obtaining the next sample to preserve its integrity.

Meanwhile, Brian and Kevin continued with their act. They embarked on a mock argument regarding the book. Brian opened it partway and suddenly slammed it shut. Kevin attempted to glance inside and Brian thwarted him. Our curiosity was piqued, not least Lanta's. She approached the table, close enough to view the book but sufficiently distant to safeguard her personal space. Brian and Kevin feigned fatigue and resolved on a truce with conditions. The book was special and could only be viewed by special people. And since everyone in the room was special, everyone present could view the book – but only if everyone agreed to it. By this time, the entire 'audience' had entered the game. I voiced my agreement. Sergeant O'Dowd, with an uncharacteristic smile, agreed. Kevin looked at Lanta. Her eyes displayed her eagerness to see the pictures in the book. She nodded enthusiastically.

Brian opened the book and asked us to identify the subject in the picture. We all chorused, "A horse!" It became clear to us that Brian was studying the girl's response. Subsequent questions were directed exclusively to Lanta. Before long, Lanta was sitting at the table beside Brian and Kevin, drinking cups of milk and leafing through the book. Brian established that Lanta could identify numerous things illustrated – polar bear, seal, walrus, gannet, puffin, various fish, snow, and ice-floes. Her answers were rendered in her melodious vowel language. He queried her about where she had previously lived and under what conditions. As always, her responses were rendered in her sing-song language. Wherever she was from, English names, or names in a form recognizable to us, did not exist. When presented with pictures of urban places, she failed to identify towns and notable buildings.

We reached the point where the game had exhausted her. Kevin granted her time to play outside. Brian explained to us that the girl was undoubtedly familiar with the Arctic. He opened the book to an article on icebergs. He indicated to us on the accompanying map that a current, the Labrador Current, flows south from the Arctic along the Labrador coast until it collides with the Gulf Stream. He pointed to Baffin Bay off Nunavut and drew his finger down the page to Sable Island.

The magazine article described the island as a wild and windswept island of sand sitting in the North Atlantic. Its iconic crescent shape emerges from the expanse of the sea where the two currents collide. It is isolated and remote and is one of Canada's furthest offshore islands. Shifting sand dunes dominate the landscape. Wild horses roam freely, and the world's biggest breeding colony of grey seals live on its extensive beaches. More than 350 vessels have been wrecked due to rough seas, fog and submerged sandbars surrounding the island, earning it the title 'Graveyard of the Atlantic'.

Brian tapped his finger on the map. "And here you have the Gulf Stream. It flows northwards from Florida along the eastern coast of America and turns eastwards – here. At about 40°N 30°W, it splits in two. The northern stream, the North Atlantic Drift crosses to Northern Europe hitting the Irish coast – here – before continuing as far as Norway." To emphasize his point, Brian traced his finger from Baffin Bay to Sable Island to the west coast of Ireland. His finger stopped at Donegal in the north-western region of Ireland. Had the map been sufficiently detailed, his finger could have rested on Maghera. "Now, March went out like a lion. Three storms in quick succession, a week apart, tore across the North Atlantic well into April. We experienced one of the fiercest storms on record. Consider what may have happened had a boat been disabled in the Labrador Current during that period."

I continued with the line of reasoning. "It would have

drifted to the vicinity of Sable Island and got picked up by the storm…"

"…crossing over the North Atlantic to flounder on the jagged coast of Ireland…"

"…and a fatigued and weakened survivor washed ashore in a near-drowned state."

Sergeant O'Dowd interjected, "And that's what happened? That's how Lanta arrived here in Maghera?"

Brian replied. "No. That's what **could** have happened. Though I can't think of any other plausible explanation."

Kevin, who was listening intently, spoke. "Are you saying that Lanta is from Nunavut in Canada?"

Brian looked at him and then glanced at the sergeant and me. "I am saying that possibly she came from Baffin Bay, either from the Canadian side or from the Greenland west coast. This is just conjecture. Keep in mind that this is based solely on geographic features – her identification of Arctic scenes and the prevailing ocean currents. There is nothing that suggests a cultural connection to any of the communities there. For example, if she is Inuk, she fails to display any skills that a 12-year-old girl would likely have – sewing or stitching; or wood carving. She has no desire to fashion footwear or familiar clothing. The social connection is missing. But this information tells me where, and in what location, to focus our inquiries. When I leave here, I will have a picture of her recorded on my smartphone. And a recording of her language. This should help in locating her place of origin, and thence, her next of kin."

Sergeant O'Dowd spoke. "So, Brian, is this all you need? Are we done here?"

"Just a few final pieces of information, and a quick look around. I see that the girl is well looked after. She is healthy and happy." He turned to address me. "You say that she is fearful of strangers?"

I answered. "She is unable to interact with people in general. So, no school, no shopping, no playmates. Currently, I am in the process of introducing her to a small group of people, just a select few. It is a delicate process and might take many months. She has a particular fear of 'men in coats'." At this, I pointed to the sergeant. "This applies to guards in uniform, even postmen. I can only deduce that she suffered some trauma from people in uniform, either actual abuse or the threat of abuse."

"That's very interesting. And it is covered in the report I received. However, I would like to learn what is omitted from the report."

"Omitted from the report? I don't know what the guards sent to you, but for my part, nothing was omitted."

"Let's examine her fear of, as she puts it, 'men in coats', which we understand refers to uniformed men and/or women. Did she express a basis for this fear?"

"Yes. But it did not make sense. She said 'Men in coats will take me away to kill me and eat me'. I think that paraphrases it accurately. The question is who are the 'men in coats'? When she refers to 'me', is she referring solely to herself or to her social group? Does she mean it literally or collectively?"

"And your conclusion?"

"Her fear is real. But what man in uniform would abduct a child to eat her? I don't buy that. I considered the possibility that 'men in coats' was a threat made by her parents to discipline her. I quickly dismissed that too. If that were the case, the threat would be rendered as a form of punishment."

"Like, 'if you don't behave, the boogeyman will get you'?"

"Something like that. However, the threat is present even when she is well-behaved and only when a uniformed person is present."

"Okay. So, it is not a disciplinary threat. What else could it be?"

"Perhaps she read or heard a scary story. And believed it."

"A Hansel and Gretel story, where the wicked witch intended to cook the children in the oven."

"Yes. That sure as hell scared me when I first heard it. I was too frightened to sleep at night. I needed a quick follow-up story of how all wicked witches were slain."

Brian continued to probe for a definitive opinion. "And your conclusion?"

"Somewhere between a scary story and a real threat of child abduction. And a hundred other possibilities in between."

"This is very disturbing. Child trafficking is a crime that we treat very seriously. It is an international crime spanning many countries. Sadly, it occurs all too frequently. I will investigate that as a possible element in the case."

"Sealskin." Kevin interrupted unexpectedly. "You didn't inquire about the sealskin."

"What about sealskin?" Brian asked.

"I asked Lanta what she wore before arriving here. She said 'skin' and a word I did not recognize at the time. Later, she pointed to a picture of a seal and uttered the same word. So, she wore sealskin."

"That reinforces the theory that she hails from the Arctic. Seal hunting and the sale of seal products are prohibited except for indigenous people living above the 53° of latitude in Canada – it is a protected right of their traditional way of life."

Sergeant O'Dowd interjected. "That's it? No other seal hunting in Canada?"

"Not quite. Outside of Inuit hunting – there are 46,000 Canadian Inuit for whom the seal is the keystone of their culture – seal hunting is permitted in a strictly-controlled hunt. Only adult seals are hunted; there is a daily limit and a seasonal limit; the designated season is short; hunters require a licence. The seal hunt is controversial. It is justified as necessary for culling the number of seals. If the seal population exceeds a healthy sustainable level, the entire herd suffers. Sometimes, where the authorized hunt fails to meet the set quota, the government undertakes an additional culling program."

"I did not know that," the sergeant remarked.

"About seal hunting?"

"No. That the seal is the keystone of Inuit culture."

Kevin picked up on the information. "All the more reason to regard Lanta as Inuit."

Brian responded, "Perhaps, or perhaps not. Regardless, it all points to Canada-Greenland."

Sergeant O'Dowd was impatient to conclude the meeting. "Well, Brian, I guess we're done. I trust the information you obtained today will solve our conundrum and settle the girl safely back to her home."

"Yes. Thank you for your cooperation. All I need now is the girl's DNA sample and I'll be off."

I asked Brian to wait while I procured the requested sample. I obtained the kit from my car and searched for Lanta. Kevin knew where she was.

"Listen," Kevin said. "She is on the clifftop crooning to the sea."

Brian and I listened. We heard vowel sounds rising and falling, carried by the wind that was blowing in from the ocean. At first, we assumed that it was the sound of the wind itself. As we neared the source, we perceived the girl looking out to sea and chanting vowels in her strange language. Brian had me pause while he recorded the girl's song.

"This is important", he said. "Songs are like social fingerprints. This should assist in identifying her cultural home."

After I obtained the saliva swabs for DNA testing, I gave one to Brian McCann of Canadian Consular Services. I gave the second one to Sergeant O'Dowd. Thereupon, both men departed at the same time. I remained behind with Kevin. Back inside the cottage, Kevin sat at the table and wrote copiously in his daily journal. I heard Lanta playing outside. I spoke to him. He appeared to be oblivious to my presence. Since he chose to ignore me, I proceeded to leave.

Then he acknowledged me. "I'll have that cup of tea now."

That's all he said. There had been no previous mention of tea, or any communication since the others left. Normally, I would have been annoyed at this. But this was Kevin, regarded as odd by many. And I was curious about his writing. I brewed a pot of tea and served him a cupful. He continued to ignore me. I set next to the fireplace and stared at the cold ashes. I directed a few comments to Kevin to test his response. There was none. Suddenly, he spoke. It could have been to himself, or to no one at all.

"Two similar unrelated items – coincidence. Three would be a series, a pattern."

I turned to face him. "You found similar unrelated items? Then they are likely related."

"A series of three or more is like a map."

"A map to pinpoint a location?"

"A map of who Lanta is; where she is from; where she is going. A profile."

"And you found a revealing series of informative facts?"

Kevin placed his pen against his mouth. He was pensive. "Information, yes. But not hard facts. A pattern, nonetheless."

I was getting impatient with him. "So? What is the pattern?"

Kevin looked at me as if he had not been aware of my presence hitherto. "What did you say?"

"I asked you about the pattern you found."

Kevin shut the journal and placed the pen on the desk. "No. I have not discovered a pattern – not yet. But when I do, I'll know."

I threw up my hands at his lack of clear reasoning.

CHAPTER NINE

THE SUMMER OF CHANGE

The month of July progressed through a pleasant summer. Both Kevin and Lanta displayed positive rehabilitation and favourable progress. I persuaded Kevin to visit the dentist. The appointment was successful despite his apparent misapprehension – not uncommon in a visit to the dentist. But he put his foot down when I suggested he meet with the barber. He insisted on keeping his long hair in a ponytail.

Lanta's progress was striking. She spent two days a week in Inver. Maura Doherty decorated a room, especially for her, 'Lanta's den', where she slept during her overnight visits. She played on the beach with the Conneely children. She was their favoured team member in their swimming races. The children learned her name and pronounced it correctly. Maura sought Sarah Conneely's advice on choosing appropriate footwear for her. Sarah understood the challenges in choosing the correct footwear for a wide-toed child and demonstrated how she overcame the problem in her household. Her 12-year-old daughter Peggy's shoes had insoles and heel guards inserted for a snug fit while allowing for wide toes. She recommended the appropriate make, brand and size, allowing for extra space for growth. Armed with this information, Maura Doherty conducted a successful shopping excursion.

She obtained a pair of lace-up wide-toes trainers. Lanta, on her part, accepted the new shoes, but would only wear them when she had to 'dress up'. Maura was amused at this. It was a reaction characteristic of the Conneely children next door.

The most remarkable development in Lanta was in her education. Thanks to Kevin's homeschooling, she was reading at fourth-class level. Her favourite book was *Irish Myths and Legends.* He ensured that she was proficient in all six curriculum subjects – Gaeilge and English, Mathematics, Social Education (History and Geography), Arts Education, Physical Education and Health Education. She still needed help with her maths, but Kevin believed that, when the school year resumed in the autumn, she could effectively enter Inver National School at the fifth-class level, appropriate for ages 11 and 12.

I cautioned Kevin about setting his heart on plans that might not materialize. I requested him to consider what will happen when Lanta is reunited with her family. Three months had elapsed since Lanta entered his life. It was apparent that Kevin had come to regard Lanta as a permanent resident and a member of his family and that reunion with her former life was becoming a remote possibility. In Ireland, Lanta was now regarded as a separated child seeking asylum and officially came under the care of the Tusla's Child and Family Agency as a refugee. I conceded that Kevin was prudent and timely in making arrangements for Lanta's care in Inver.

I continued to appraise Sergeant O'Dowd of Lanta's progress. I met with him in the Garda station. I informed him of the plans to relocate the girl to Inver where she would assume a normal life for a 12-year-old girl. He advised me that Tusla would assess the suitability of the proposal. Permission would ultimately rest with them. After 90 days, if the girl was not repatriated to her home, she would receive temporary residency status in Ireland. This would provide her with an identity and certain rights comparable to underage Irish citizens. It would also place her in foster care. I had no direct line of communication with Tusla. Sergeant O'Dowd was my go-between. In my opinion, Kevin's proposal was in the best interests of the girl. I was optimistic that, when the proposal was accepted, Lanta would move in with foster parents Padraig and Maura Doherty. She would then embark on a normal childhood and effectively mature into adulthood in a family and community environment.

I asked the sergeant for an update on his lost-child inquiries. So far, none of the leads on missing children fitted Lanta's profile. Her details and picture had been extensively circulated to police services internationally but to no avail. She was currently listed on the Garda website's 'Missing Persons' section. To increase awareness, and in consultation with Tusla, a national appeal on television was imminent, supported by a picture of the sorrowful waif. This would invite help from the general public. Of course, her whereabouts would not be disclosed other than to state that she was 'in the care of Child Protection and Welfare'. The Canadian inquiry, the only promising lead, was 'inconclusive'. Brian McCann, the sergeant informed me, needed additional data for the investigation and wanted my input. To this end. the sergeant had provided the Canadian Consulate with my phone number and email address. I wondered to what extent the Canadian lead had progressed or if it too had resulted in a dead-end.

On the following day, I received a phone call from Brian McCann. I asked him about the 'inconclusive' results of the inquiry. "Were you able to trace the girl back to one of the Inuit communities?"

"None of the Inuit or Dene communities in Canada or Greenland report a missing child fitting her description – there are nine Inuit groups in Canada and there are Dene Nation communities in Northwest Territories. We circulated her picture and samples of her voice. Her language is definitely not Inuit – not Inuvialuktun, Inuinnaqtuun or any of the different dialects of Inuktitut. Furthermore, her features are non-Inuit. We got the same non-results from the Dene Nation farther west. Other than unsubstantiated speculation on ocean currents bringing her across the North Atlantic, there is nothing to connect the girl to any Inuit or indigenous community."

"Hold on, Brian. She could be of mixed race. Surely the DNA test would indicate her race."

"Not so. Genetic testing can point you to your ancestry, but not to race."

"Yes, of course. There is a difference."

"Anyway, that brings up an important issue. Your sample was either contaminated or degraded to the point that an accurate reading was unobtainable."

"I don't believe it. That's the second time that happened. My plastic pouches must be the problem. I'll get a new batch of bags and conduct another test."

"Great. That's what I need."

"So, tell me, how badly degraded was the sample?"

"I don't know. The lab asked about the donor. I

informed them that it was a 12-year-old girl. I spoke to the lab tech off the record, I must add. He laughed and told me that the state of the sample was so contaminated that he could not confirm if it came from a girl of any age."

"So, you came up empty-handed?"

"No, Fred, not quite. Here's the strange thing. One community at Baffin Bay has an elder who recognized Lanta's song. He does not recognize the language of the song, but the tune is familiar to him. He is unable to remember exactly where he heard it, except that he was hunting off Baffin Island at the time. That was a few years ago. He heard the song but was unable to see the singer. When he went to investigate the hidden vocalist, there was no one there. He thought at the time that he had mistaken the sound of the wind for singing. So, he put the matter out of his head. That is until he heard my recording of it."

"As you say, Brian, that's strange. So, the girl is from Baffin Island but is not from any known community there? Is that what you're saying?"

"This is what we know. The girl is likely from the Arctic, not necessarily from Baffin Island. But she is **not** from any indigenous group. Her language, if it is a language at all, is unknown; her features are foreign to any known community; she does not display any skills or characteristics that would place her in an identifiable culture. We extended our inquiries to Alaska and to Greenland. We exhausted all leads. The official conclusion, one that we shared with your police through diplomatic channels, is 'inconclusive'."

I thought for a moment. 'Inconclusive' sounded much like 'dead-end'. "Okay," I said. "For what it is worth, I will conduct another DNA test and send you the results."

"Thanks, Fred. Sorry about the failure to reach a satisfying outcome. It is disappointing."

"Well, we can only do what we can do. Thanks, Brian. I'll be in touch."

The call ended. I was puzzled more than ever about Lanta's origin. How could someone not report her missing? And what connection had she to Baffin Island? How remote was her community that her language is unknown and unidentifiable?

I drove to Kevin's cottage to appraise him of the updated report. And to obtain yet another fresh DNA sample from Lanta. I regretted my previous inability to obtain a blood sample from her. Tusla had already contacted me regarding this. Blood tests were required for the completion of the medical tests. They were necessary and they were overdue. A blood test could provide invaluable information, perhaps the very information required to solve the mystery of her origin. I resolved to obtain the overdue blood sample as soon as possible. How was I to draw blood from her without traumatizing her? I was a doctor. I'd find a way. Inside the cottage, Kevin was busy writing. He was grumpy and uncommunicative as he focused on his task. I deduced that Lanta was playing somewhere alone. Kevin, by this time, permitted her free time unsupervised. I wondered if that was prudent considering her love of swimming in the ocean. Kevin's opinion was that if she could survive a storm at sea then surely she is safe in calm water close to shore.

I brewed a pot of tea. I presented a cup of the beverage to Kevin. He took it from me without saying a word. I peered at his writing. It was not in a language I recognized. It was comprised of cryptic symbols and curves mixed-up with letters and numerals of varying sizes. Kevin spoke. He appeared to address his task but spoke aloud for my benefit.

"Lanta speaks English in a strange manner. Actually, she speaks three different forms of English. 'Book-English' is written. When spoken, it is rendered without tone or expression. It is a mute language, not really a language at all – more a set of instructions. 'Spoken English' relies on the tone of the voice and works in conjunction with gestures, visual shapes and melodies. Spoken English can be very poor, or very rich, depending on the quality of the speaker or the level of understanding of the one to whom it is addressed. Lastly, there is the English that lacks adequately descriptive words. Here, Lanta inserts contributions from her native language to form her unique form of English – Songlish." He paused at this point in his description. Then he appeared to have an insight. "It's the grammar, you know. English has a rich vocabulary of words but is defective in grammatical accuracy. In Lanta's view, the word 'you' is spoken differently to indicate singular or plural, nominative, imperative or dative cases. The meaning is conveyed by context and tonal expression – as it should be. By contrast, 'I', 'me', 'we' and 'us' is a cumbersome use of what should be a single word. And tenses. There is only one tense. The shape of the diphthong is all that is required to convey the meaning – like 'read' in the present and 'read' in the past. It's the same word; you just say it differently. At least according to Lanta."

I interrupted him. This discourse was too tedious for me. "So, what is your writing? Surely, it is not English."

Kevin laughed. "I am playing with the possibility of writing a language with sounds and rhythm."

"Is that possible?"

"Of course. Consider the score for a stage musical. It has words, music, singing, dancing, costumes and a whole lot more."

"Ah, yes," I answered with little enthusiasm. I now wished that I had not interrupted his work and broken his silence. I departed from the cottage to look for Lanta. Or maybe it was to seek relief from Kevin's dissertation. I exited through the doorway. From outside, I heard Kevin's voice still speaking to me, or to himself or to no one at all.

It was an unusually calm day. The ocean breeze, moist and salty, wafted gently up the cliff face. I heard Lanta's voice. She was singing one of her vowel songs with no recognizable rhythm or key. What was different this time, was the short duration of each phrase. She was close by, partly hidden by the heather at the cliff edge. Her yellow sundress betrayed her location. She did not notice my approach. She focused her attention on the inlet below. I walked to the cliff edge. I peered down to see what was of interest to her. The tide was out and a colony of seals lay on the exposed sandbar, basking in the sun. At each phrase of Lanta's song, the seals raised their heads and bobbed gently. It was strange and wonderful. They seemed to answer her song – a phrase from the girl followed by a response from the seals. Up to then, I understood that seals emitted a monotonous hoarse bark and nothing more. This is not so. I later learned that they vocalize underwater with a peak frequency of 1.2 kHz. The seals on the sandbar produced a wide variety of in-air vocalizations – short barks, tonal honks, grunts, growls, roars, moans and pup-calls. I thought at first that Lanta's singing disturbed their rest. But as I watched and listened, the girl and the seals seemed to be in a singing conversation. I could not tell if it was a true two-way communication, or if the seals just reacted to her vowel sounds. It is not unusual for a mammal to react to a human voice. Dogs and cats interact vocally with humans, so why not marine mammals? It was fascinating to observe. I wondered where Lanta acquired this rare skill. Baffin Bay, perhaps? I decided not to disturb the girl. And I was reluctant to re-enter the cottage to be subjected to Kevin's tiresome explanation on how to write a spoken language in musical form. I decided to remain on the cliff top and enjoy the tranquillity of the day. I had intended to obtain a fresh saliva swab for DNA testing. I postponed it for later.

Lanta unexpectedly ceased singing mid-phrase and fell

silent. She heard something intrusive. I listened and heard it too – the sound of three cars on the coast road below. Three concurrent cars on the isolated road was a rare occurrence. We deduced from the sound that the cars had turned off the road and were approaching the cottage. In keeping with her customary behaviour, Lanta retreated from the cliff edge and entered the cottage to hide from the intruders. I, on the other hand, walked to the front of the cottage to meet the arriving cars. I knew that Kevin would not entertain this number of simultaneous callers. His parents, whenever they came, arrived in a single car. So too, did the sergeant – and he always phoned ahead. Three unexpected cars signalled trouble.

I placed myself, like a sentry, at the entrance to the cottage. The lead car contained Sergeant O'Dowd. He strode officiously to the cottage door. He was in garda uniform. I was disturbed by this. He was aware of Lanta's fear of uniformed people. I addressed him. "Sergeant O'Dowd, what brings you here…"

"Stand aside. I am on official police business," he interrupted me briskly.

The occupants of the second car approached us. It was Doctor Kathleen McBrearty, the psychologist from Tusla, and a younger man whom she referred to as 'medic'.

I held my ground. The third car was a garda patrol car. Two uniformed officers, one male and one female, exited the car and approached us. This was an ominous contingent. I spoke firmly to the sergeant. "If your 'police business' pertains to one of my patients, it is my business too. Why are you here, unannounced and with such portentous force?"

Doctor McBrearty prompted him. "Tell him. And then get on with it."

The sergeant coughed. He resented the psychologist's sharp and intrusive remark. He continued to address me. "We have a court order to acquire the unnamed child resident within…:

"Her name is 'Lanta'," I interrupted hotly.

"…the abode of Kevin Doherty of Maghera, County Donegal. The said child is to be placed in the care of the Child and Family Agency forthwith by court order under the Child Care Act 1991. Now stand aside or I will have you arrested for interference with police business." He leaned closer and lowered his voice. "This is an unpleasant task for me. But it is the law and I must enforce the order. Now don't make it more difficult than it already is."

I held my silence. I also held my ground. From inside

the cottage, I heard the commotion. Lanta had spied the uniformed officers. She was shouting in her native language interspersed with English. "The men in coats are here. Don't let them in, Kevin! Save me! They are here to take me away to eat me. Save me! Save me!"

The sounds were audible to the group outside. Sergeant O'Dowd gestured to the two gardai. One went to the rear of the cottage, presumably to foil any attempt by the girl to flee through the back door. He pushed me firmly but gently aside and had the second garda enter the house. Then the sergeant and the remainder of the party hastily entered the cottage.

Kevin shouted, "Run, Lanta, run!" A chaotic struggle ensued – the sound of toppling chairs, the crash of falling dishes. The girl shrieked again and again. Someone shouted, "She is making for the back door. Grab her!" The garda at the back door intercepted her and nabbed her. It took two officers to restrain her, holding her by her wrists and ankles. She shrieked and kicked and wriggled. Thus, they carried her to the front of the house. It was clear that the child was frantic and was in danger of injuring herself.

Doctor McBrearty turned to the medic and instructed him to administer a sedative. He had been forewarned and was prepared for this. As he steadied the syringe, I launched myself against his body toppling him. The psychologist, standing alongside, tumbled in the process. Simultaneously, Kevin hurled himself at the two guards. In the multiple collision – Kevin against the guards, the falling medic and psychologist and me – bodies piled upon bodies. In the confusion, Lanta broke free. She ran. Only Sergeant O'Dowd was still standing unscathed. He dashed to the girl but tripped on the tangle of arms and legs. In his attempt to grab hold of Lanta, the girl slipped like an eel out of his grasp. In doing so, she left the sergeant holding an empty yellow sundress. Lanta ran from the house and across the clifftop, leaping over mounds of heather. The two gardai recovered quickly and ran in pursuit. The guards were athletic and fit. They rapidly closed the gap on the fleeing girl. They expected her to run along the clifftop. Instead, she surprised them by jumping off the edge of the cliff. There was an audible intake of breath from the entire group. We feared that the girl had fallen to her death, smashed on the rocks below. But no, we still heard the running sound of her bare feet.

One of the guards shouted, "Look! There she is. She's on a path. She's descending the cliff."

Lanta had not jumped over the cliff as we had feared, she had launched herself onto the steep pathway on the cliff face. She executed the descent nimbly and swiftly on the familiar pathway. The guards were unacquainted with the cliff. They descended cautiously. Lanta increased her distance substantially. She reached the secluded cove well ahead of them, whereupon she dived into the shallow water of the incoming tide. The sergeant and Kevin followed the pursuing gardai down the cliff face. They spotted the girl in the water, swimming strongly away from the shore.

Kevin shouted after her, "Swim away! Swim far away!"

"Quick!" the sergeant said to his two officers. "Into the boat."

The three guards pushed Kevin's light boat into the water and started the engine. The boat sped across the inlet, much faster than Lanta could swim. But once again, she thwarted their attempt to capture her. Instead of swimming toward open water, she reached the sandbar. The basking seals were disturbed by the tumult. They plunged into the water on the ocean side. Lanta ran across the sandbar and leapt into the water amidst the pod of swimming seals. An argument ensued amongst the guards as to which action they should take – carry the light boat across the sandbar and relaunch on the ocean side, or, go around by way of the coastal channel of the incoming tide. They decided to go by way of the channel.

Meanwhile, Kevin returned to the clifftop, where he

and I and the Tusla agents viewed the activity below. We peered intently at the swimmers in the water. We could distinguish the seals. But there was no sign of Lanta. I asked, to no one in particular, "Do you see her? I don't think she resurfaced from her dive."

The Tusla agents concurred. "You are correct. She did not resurface. She went into the water and did not reappear."

Kevin mumbled in a low voice, "She is with the seals. Look out there." He pointed to where the pod of seals was swimming towards the open ocean.

Other than Kevin, no one could identify the girl among the seals. The ocean was rough and the currents were wild. Most likely she was sucked under after her dive. Nobody could swim against the incoming tide in the currents off the headland. There was a slim chance that she could ride the incoming tide back inland, as she did on the day of the storm. Could she have tricked us into believing that she was swimming out to sea, when in fact, she had turned back? Perhaps she did not jump into the water with the seals after all. Maybe she jumped back to the landward side of the sandbar when she saw the boat proceeding to the ocean. At the time, we were distracted by the activity of the seals. I looked at the sandbar to distinguish her footprints to determine where she re-entered the water. But by then the water of the incoming tide was washing over the sand and had obliterated the tracks. We peered along the rocky shore to see if she had turned around and proceeded back. There was no sign of her either on the water or on the shore. Other than Kevin, we unanimously concluded that she dived into the water on the oceanside of the sandbar and she did not resurface.

Meanwhile, the boat was in pursuit of her among the pod of seals. The view from the boat was obscured by the swells of the sea. Once clear of the sandbar, the boat lurched precariously on the swells. The occupants argued. They glimpsed the girl, or maybe they didn't. They were unable to distinguish the true identity of what was swimming amid the pod of seals. "Is that her?" "No, that's a seal!" "Are you sure?" "I can't tell!" Whenever the boat entered a trough between the swells, their view was obscured. And whenever a seal swam in a trough, it was likewise hidden. Locating anything in the heaving sea was impossible. A swell hit the boat broadside. Water washed aboard. The three guards were drenched. They struggled to keep the bow towards the incoming swells. As a result, they proceeded in the wrong direction and entered rougher waters. Fearful of their perilous state, they turned the boat around. Another swell washed aboard. The boat was in danger of sinking. The guards used their caps to bail out the water. Fatigued and saturated, they made it back to calm waters. They were thankful that they had failed to catch the girl out at sea. A fourth person aboard would have swamped the unstable craft. The result would have been disastrous. They would have perished for sure in the turbulent ocean swells.

Once back on land, Sergeant O'Dowd informed Search and Rescue of the tragedy. He advised that the undertaking would be for a search and recovery. It was too late for rescue. An alert was issued. We were downcast. The three gardai and the two Tusla officials agreed that the incident was an unforeseen tragedy. I bit my tongue. It was not wholly unforeseen. In my opinion, the entire affair was handled recklessly with little regard for the girl's well-being. Of all the possible outcomes, each one would have been tragic; this was just the worst.

CHAPTER TEN

SONG OF THE SEA

When the gardai and Tusla officials left, I remained at the cottage. I felt helpless, but I could not bring myself to leave the place of misfortune. I sat in silence by the dead fire. Kevin worked at his desk writing copiously. Every few minutes he muttered to himself. "She is not dead. She is with the seals." I pitied him. He was in denial. I feared that he was losing his grip on reality and would fall into another state of depression. The progress of the previous months would be erased and his new state would be worse than before. I decided to stay with him until the following day. I did not trust him to be alone at this time.

I awoke at dawn. I was still propped up in the chair by the fireplace. I was stiff from sleeping in a sitting position. I stretched and yawned and limbered up my joints. Kevin was still at his desk. I guessed that he had spent the entire night there, writing in his journal. I did not detect any sign of grief in him. Was he taking comfort in a mundane routine exercise? This was not a good sign. I stirred and walked around. I noticed Lanta's yellow dress, her favourite, lying on the floor. It was torn at one side. I lifted it, folded it gently and placed it on her bed. I don't know why I did it. It seemed like the right thing to do. Afterwards, I walked as far as the gatepost where I collected the morning's supply of milk and eggs. Back in the cottage, I prepared breakfast. I served Kevin a cup of tea and a plate of fried eggs, baked beans and sardines. In my opinion, it was an unappetizing meal, but Kevin liked it. I left him to his meal and his writing. I promised to phone him throughout the day. He grunted in acknowledgement. Then, I drove back to town. I phoned him later but he did not pick up. I remembered that, without electricity, Kevin charged his mobile phone while driving his car. I assumed that his phone battery was dead, as was often the case, and that he was unable to answer his calls.

The next day, I visited him. Except that he was not at the cottage. I noticed that he had neglected to collect his morning's milk and eggs. His car was parked in its usual spot. His phone was lying on the desk. I checked it. The battery was dead – no surprise. Assuming that he was out walking on the heath, I made breakfast of tea and boiled eggs and awaited his return. An hour later, I was anxious. I went in search of him. He was not visible on the headland. I scanned the inlet from the clifftop. There was no sign of him aboard his boat. I walked along the cliff path to the caves and descended to Maghera Beach, to the area hidden from view from the cottage. It was deserted. I walked along the line of wrack at the high-tide mark. I saw flotsam of wrecked fishing gear that had washed ashore, but no sign of Kevin. I returned to the pathway over the caves and returned to the cottage. This time, I descended the path to Kevin's secluded cove. I was surprised to find the boat gone. If the boat was gone and it was not visible in the inlet, could Kevin have ventured out to sea? He knew that his boat was not seaworthy. He would not venture beyond the shelter of the bay. But I was worried that in his present state of mind he may have acted irresponsibly. I searched my mind for an explanation for the boat's absence. It came to me. I surmised that when the guards returned the boat to the cove, they beached it above the waterline. However, it was half-tide at the time and the boat was beached on dry land but below the high-tide level. Later, the incoming tide floated the boat and it drifted away. And after the tide turned, the outgoing current carried the boat out to sea. That was the most likely explanation. I felt better. I returned to the cottage. Kevin would turn up sooner or later during the day – or so I hoped.

Throughout the day I busied myself in the house. I read Kevin's journal – the decipherable parts. I tidied the kitchen and the other rooms. In doing so, I discovered that Lanta's yellow dress was missing. I checked through her belongings and realized that she did not have any personal items – and never had – except for the items presented to her by Maura Doherty. What were they? The lace-up trainers and undergarments. And these were missing too. In fact, there were none of

Lanta's possessions in the house. It was as if she had never been here or even existed. I shivered at the thought. Of course, she had been here. I treated her as my patient. And Kevin's journal can attest to it.

At mid-afternoon, I was deep in thought. My thoughts were wandering, taking me to unfamiliar places. I heard a distant sound. It was Lanta's Song of the Sea. I shook myself to an alert state. The song remained audible, albeit faint and distant. I shivered. Kevin, I suspected, had a fragile grip on reality. Was I also losing my grip? I ran outside and hurried to the source of the sound, the place from where the song emanated. I slowed my pace to a walk. I hesitated. I was afraid to face the source of the plaintive vowels rising and falling mournfully from the headland. Could it be Lanta? I berated myself for my foolishness. It was most likely Kevin on the headland. He had learned Lanta's Song of the Sea and was intoning it in a falsetto voice. With this understanding, I renewed my journey to the source of the sound. But when I reached the cliff-edge location, there was no one there and the sound ceased. I remembered that Brian McCann described the same phenomenon. It also happened to the Inuit elder on Baffin Island. Once again, I experienced a shiver. This was an eerie experience. I slowly retreated backwards from the cliff edge. The sound recommenced, although there was no one there. I fell to my knees and laughed in relief. All along, I had been listening to the sound of the ocean breeze whistling through the heather at the cliff edge. But how did the breeze know Lanta's song? Of course, it was the other way around. Lanta's song was inspired by the sound of the wind blowing inland from the sea. It truly was a 'Song of the Sea'.

I returned to the cottage with mixed feelings. I was relieved at discovering a rational explanation for the song I heard. But the circumstances were peculiar. And Kevin was still absent without explanation. I brewed a pot of tea, hoping that the beverage would relax me. I, a doctor, consumed caffeine to relax. It was indicative of my unsettled state.

My phone rang. I jumped in alarm. A ringing phone is not usually disturbing. I was on edge. I accepted the call. It was Sergeant O'Dowd.

"Doctor Harrison?"

"Yes."

"Sergeant O'Dowd, here. Listen, I'm trying to get in touch with Kevin Doherty, but he is not answering his phone. Do you know where he is?"

"No, I don't know exactly where he is. I am at his cottage now. His phone is here – dead battery, as usual. He can't be far away. His car is parked outside. Why do you ask?"

"The Search and Rescue Unit…"

"What? They found Lanta?"

"No. They are still searching for her. But they found something else of interest – an empty boat floating in Gweebarra Bay, not far from Dooey Beach. It was pushed in by the prevailing winds. So, Doctor, if you are at Doherty's cottage now, see if his boat is there. The one we found looks like his."

I experienced another unwelcome shiver. "I don't need to look. I know with certainty that Kevin's boat is not here, or anywhere in Maghera Bay. I already looked for it. I figured that it drifted away in the tide after your officers beached it in the cove. I don't think they placed it high enough above the high-tide mark."

"That's possible. I remember tipping the boat to empty it of water. But, I don't remember placing it above the high-tide mark. So, you think it just drifted away in the outgoing tide and the prevailing wind blew it into Gweebarra Bay? That's very likely."

"I think that's the most reasonable explanation." Inwardly, I considered a more ominous explanation, I suppressed it.

"Anyway, it might not be Doherty's boat at all. This boat, like his, has no markings. The only identifiable item found on board was a pair of shoes – ratty deck shoes with a tear at the side. Could be castoff shoes."

"A tear on the right of the toe of the right shoe? Mended, unsuccessfully, with black pitch?"

"That's right."

"Kevin's boating shoes. That means that Kevin was out in the boat in Gweebarra Bay."

"Hold on, Fred. Don't jump to conclusions. Kevin Doherty's boat may have drifted away like you say, unmanned. Except… Except that we tipped everything out of the boat with the water. How did his shoes subsequently get on board?"

"Kevin was in the boat afterwards."

"Lord, I believe we have another situation for Search and Rescue." Sergeant O'Dowd terminated the call before I speculated any further.

Alone in the cottage, I paced back and forth in anxiety. Could Kevin have committed suicide, I wondered? Yes, he was in denial of Lanta's death. But he did not display derealization or the risk of suicidal thoughts or actions. If he were to take his life, would he not simply throw himself off the cliff and into the tidal currents? Why go to the trouble of sailing out to sea? If it were suicide, there would be a suicide note. I laughed aloud at this. Suicide notes are not always in evidence. That only happens in fictional stories. This was real life. I laughed again. What was 'real' in Kevin's life? Or in the events of the past three months? Still, suicide does not come out of the blue. There had to be clues.

I searched through Kevin's desk in the hope of finding an answer. I spied the journal. Kevin was writing reams in his journal on the night before his disappearance. This might contain a substitute for his 'suicide note'. I sat at the desk and proceeded to read the recent entries. Only a third of the text was intelligible. I encountered a remark written in the margin in red ink. It referred to 'three items that form a pattern' – the seals at Baffin Island, the seals at Sable Island and the seals at Raoninish (Irish for 'Seal-Island'). I had no recollection of any previous reference to Roaninish. I don't know where it came from, but I sure knew where it was headed. Kevin, in denying Lanta's death, said, 'She is not dead; she is with the seals'. And he referred to a pattern as 'a map'. There is a seal colony on Roaninish. It lies a mere 14 kilometres due north of Knockfola headland, at the mouth of Gweebarra Bay. I walked to the backdoor and looked out to sea. Roaninish was visible from the cottage – a flat rocky inhospitable islet.

A daunting environment – except for seals. With shaking hands, I phoned Sergeant O'Dowd. It took me three attempts to correctly enter his number. He answered immediately. I breathed a sigh of relief.

He spoke. "Doctor Harrison? I recognized your caller identification..."

I interrupted him. "Roaninish!" I was panting.

"Roaninish? What about Roaninish?"

"That's where he went – or attempted to."

"Who?"

"Kevin, of course. I saw it in his journal."

"He left a note?"

"Not a note. More of a message. Do you remember him saying that Lanta was not dead; that she was with the seals?"

"Well, yes."

"In his daily journal he wrote a reference to a pattern; he referred to it as a map. Listen. 'Baffin Island', 'Sable Island', 'Roaninish'. Sergeant, these are sites of significant seal colonies."

"Roaninish? It's a barren isle. There's nothing there, not even a landing spot for a boat. However, it has a seal colony at certain times of the year – like now. Look, Fred, I'm on it. I'll contact Search and Rescue right away." He terminated the call.

I needed to relax. I brewed a pot of tea – double strength. Extra caffeine to relax. I laughed at the irony. Later, I mused over the significance of Lanta's missing belongings. Did Kevin hope to reunite with her and restore them to her? I spied, on the desk, a copy of *Irish Myths and Legends.* It had been Lanta's favourite book. Was this the only thing remaining in the house that had a connection to her? I noticed a bookmark – perhaps marking the last page she had read. Or, possibly it was Kevin's bookmark. I opened the book to the marked page. It was a tale of a selkie. At the end of the tale, the page described the source and tradition of the story. This reference was underlined in red:

In Celtic mythology, selkies (or selkie folk, meaning 'seal folk') are mythological beings capable of therianthropy, changing from seal to human. There is the tradition that the Conneely clan of Connemara was descended from seals, and it was offensive for them to hunt or harm the animals. Selkies have a particular connection with Roaninish (Rón-inis, meaning 'seal island') outside Gweebarra Bay off the west coast of

Donegal in Ulster.

I was shocked upon reading this. I reflected on Lanta's peculiar behaviour and her understanding of what she encountered. She had a dread of 'men in coats'. Seal hunters? This was too fantastic to be credible. Selkies exist solely in mythology. But, perhaps Kevin, whose grip on reality was fragile, believed it to be true. He did not display grief at Lanta's disappearance, because he truly believed that she joined the pod of seals. What I perceived in Kevin's demeanour was determination, not simply denial.

I urgently needed confirmation on the only remaining personal item of Lanta – her DNA results. I phoned Brian McCann. I trembled so vigorously that I was unable to enter his number. I scrolled to his most recent call and hit 'reply'. I listened to his phone ringing. "Pick up! Pick up!" I shouted at the device. He answered on the fourth ring. I did not wait for him to speak. I shouted "Brian? Is that you?"

"Yes. Who is this?"

"Fred Harrison."

"Oh, hello Fred. If you are inquiring about any further progress…"

"Brian, the DNA test. You told me that it was

contaminated; that it was not from a 12-year-old girl."

"No. Not literally. The lab tech was joking. Hey, it was off the record. This is not in the report."

"How did he describe it?"

"He did not say. He was just joking about the degree of contamination."

"WHAT DID HE SAY in the joke?"

"He laughed and said that we must have mixed up the sample with one from a marine mammal. But it was a joke. An insensitive joke, I admit. Don't give it any credence."

"He said 'marine mammal'?"

"Yes…"

I disconnected the call. I sat at Kevin's desk. I needed to gather my thoughts. I read through his journal from his first entry to his last. Much of the later entries were indecipherable. I scoured my memory for information on Lanta. And I wrote, and wrote, and wrote. When I finished writing, I was exhausted. My phone was dead. How long had I been here, writing in solitude in Kevin's remote cottage accompanied solely by the sounds of the crashing waves and the plaintive moaning of the Song of the Sea? A day? Or more? I evaluated the content of my manuscript. I could not state the inescapable conclusion. I dared not even think it. It was implied clearly, nevertheless.

*   *   *   *   *   *   *

I conclude my account as follows:

The story of Lanta is finished. I will place my written account of the life of Lanta with Kevin's journal. These two documents I will seal in an envelope and conceal in the cottage. I will choose a place that Sergeant O'Dowd will not discover. Once sealed and secreted, the recorded events will be erased from my memory. They never occurred. This technique of memory-purging worked for me in Afghanistan; it will work for me here in Ireland. The only thing I am unable to lock away is the recurring Song of the Sea.

*   *   *   *   *   *   *

I, Frederick Harrison, being of sound mind, attest to the truthfulness of this document and, in so doing, place my signature as my pledge.

Fred Harrison

Dated this 31 day of July 2022, at Maghera in the County of Donegal, Ireland

Acknowledgements:

gov.ie – Website of The Government of Ireland, Department of Children, Equality, Disability, Integration and Youth

irelandsloreandtales.com – website of 'Ireland's Lore and Tales', issue November 17, 2020, folklore of selkies, selkie folk (meaning 'seal folk')

pc.gc.ca – Government of Canada website, National Parks, data on Sable Island National Park Reserve

verywellmind.com – Enochlophobia, symptoms and treatment

Wikipedia – Gulf Stream and North Atlantic Drift

ABOUT THE AUTHOR

Fergus Patrick Egan was born in 1945 in Donegal in the northwest of Ireland where he spent his early life. He spent 20 years in retail banking, including 10 years in Toronto, Canada. Over the course of 30 years, he worked in the Canadian travel industry. He currently resides in Ontario, Canada.

Other books by the author:

Black Donnelly, Rats and Pigs

The Coin and the Key

The Famine Field

Dorinda Trapper of Red Rapids

Field of Endeavour and Death